you will see mountains
and seas in those eyes

you will see mountains and seas in those eyes

janice simpson

Apsley Press

Published by Apsley Press

© Janice Simpson 2024

First published 2024

National Library of Australia Cataloguing-in-Publication entry

Creator: Simpson, Janice 1951 - author

Title: you will see mountains and seas in those eyes / Janice Simpson

ISBN: 978-0-6459158-2-2 (paperback)

ISBN: 978-0-6459158-3-9 (e-book)

Fiction

www.janicesimpson.com

CONTENTS

For Des

Luna Park

I'm in my room when I hear them come in the gate. They wait on the porch while Mum fiddles with her keys and when she finds them, she says, 'Here they are, the little buggers,' and she pokes the bunch of keys around until the right one slips in the keyhole and she turns the lock and opens the door. She steps into the hallway. She says in this really loud voice that's meant to be quiet, 'Come in, everyone's asleep, so come on in.'

I hear Mum's heels on the floorboards in the hall, 'Click, click, click, click,' and next I hear her crash into the wall near my bedroom door. She tries to turn on the hallway light and I can hear her patting the wall where she thinks the switch is. Someone giggles and Mum says, 'SHHHHH.' If we were asleep we'd be awake by now, what with the click, click, click, click and the crash into the wall and the really noisy shhhhh. Another set of heels follow her down the hall, 'Click, click, click, click,' and then two, maybe three, other sorts of shoes go down after.

Mum doesn't know it yet, but my brother's in my room tonight and it's warm with the two of us in the bed. I open my eyes a squeak and he's looking at me. I've got greeny bluey grey eyes but his are pure brown like cows' eyes. I can't see the brown right now because it's dark in my room, but I know his eyes are brown even though I can only see the white bits.

'Is that Mum?' he says.

'Yep,' I say. 'Go back to sleep now. We're going to Luna Park tomorrow, remember, so you need to be as shiny as a new pin in the morning.'

'Okay,' he says and snuggles closer and puts his small hot hand on my cheek. 'What's a new pin?' he says, and then he lifts his head and gives me a butterfly kiss. I put my arm around him and hold him tight and rub his tummy. He starts to breathe his sleep breaths and I let go a bit and stop the rubbing.

'Wine or gin, all there is in the house,' Mum says. She must have taken off her shoes because there's no more clicking, just the sound of the drinks cupboard opening and closing, and the door of the crystal cabinet hitting the chair that's always beside it and is always too close. 'Fuck,' she says. Same as what she says every time the door hits the chair. I don't think Mum's trying to be quiet now. She thinks that because my room is at the front of the house I can't hear things at the back of the house. But I can.

Like the night I heard Dad say, 'Fuck off, Susan,' and then he slammed their bedroom door and the next morning he acted kind to Danny and me but by night-time he was gone. He said he was going away to Sydney for a week to work, but he didn't, because I saw him walk past the butcher's shop three days later when Mum and Danny and me were buying sausages for tea. She didn't see him, though.

I didn't like it when Dad said 'fuck off' to Mum. But sometimes Mum says it to me now when she's really tired because she's been up all night and we're meant to be going somewhere for an outing on Sunday and she's got mascara under her eyes and down her cheeks and she smells of perfume and smoke and her clothes are on all funny, not like when she went out, and she says, 'Get breakfast yourself, I'm too tired.' And when I ask when we're going and what clothes will I get Danny into, she tells me, 'You can't even get breakfast for yourself and Danny, and that washing is still in the laundry and the TV's been keeping me awake since you two got up god knows when, so why should I take you out? So fuck off, the pair of you, I'm tired and it's just not going to happen today.'

I roll over a bit. Mum's still down the back and I can hear talking and laughing and someone goes outside onto the deck because I can hear the legs on the outdoor chairs scraping the tiles. It's cold tonight. I wouldn't go out on the deck. I think they must be smoking out there. I'll know in the morning because I'll see the butts all over the lawn when I get Buster out of the shed where he sleeps, because Mum won't let him stay inside.

Then I hear another crash and a voice I don't know says, 'Fuck,' and then Mum says, 'No worries, only a broken glass. More worried about the wine, given it's in short supply,' and they all laugh as if she's the funniest person on earth.

Sometimes Mum is funny and she tells us jokes like, how do you sell a duck to a deaf person, and she waits a bit before she shouts, WANNA BUY A DUCK, and next she laughs and that just makes Danny and me laugh harder, even though she's told us that joke hundreds of times.

I think about going back to sleep. I'm not sure what the time it is but I guess it must be about three. Still time for Mum to go to bed and be okay for us to go to Luna Park. I plan how I'll get up and dress Danny and after that get us breakfast, but not eggs because I might make too much noise beating them, so probably toast and jam, and I'll keep the TV down really low so Mum won't hear and at about half past ten or eleven I can ring her mobile from the wall phone and she'll wake up with the music, and I won't answer but she will, then I'll come in with a mug of tea and she'll say, God, I need that tea, and smile at me and say, What would I do without you, and Do you and Danny still want to go to Luna Park today, and I'll say, Sure Mum, we're practically ready to go. Can I get you anything or do anything while you get ready, and she'll say, No, love, I'll just drink this before I jump into the shower and we can be there by lunch, and then, because she's smiling and drinking her tea, she'll say, How would you like to get lunch down in Acland Street before we go into the Park?

Then I hear a different noise, like someone crying. Mum says fuck off. She says it again, and again, 'Fuck off. Go on, fuck off. Fuck off,' she says, sort of like a song. Footsteps come up the hallway towards my room. I pull the doona up and cover Danny's head and roll towards him and hold him tight so he'll just think it's a dream if he thinks it's anything at all. It's better if Danny's sleeping when Mum starts crying because when Mum cries, usually Danny does too, and straight away he starts asking for Dad and that makes Mum bawl even more, and I can't do anything when Mum cries. The front door opens and someone goes out and shuts the door behind them. 'Don't worry about him. He only wants one thing,' someone says

I wonder who only wants one thing, and if it was me, what one thing would I want. I go through stuff in my head. I want to creep out the back door as soon as it's morning and get Buster and take him to the park. I want to put on my new black jeans and the belt Dad gave me for my birthday and I want to put all my dirty clothes and Danny's in the machine and remember to close the laundry door so the machine doesn't wake Mum. I want Danny to sleep so he's as bright as a new pin. I want to eat two slices of toast with lots of jam and butter and I want to make a really good cup of tea for Mum and take it in to her and kiss her, and then she'll hug me. Like I'm hugging Danny right now, tight and warm like a python. But most of all, when Mum wakes up, I want her to remember we're going to Luna Park today.

Tying Knots

The little fat dog sprawls on the wooden deck. The autumn sun soaks into his brown-splotched belly. His tail is long gone, only a short stump left to wag out his pleasure. He isn't a bad dog. But he isn't an entirely good dog either. Once he nipped the kid next door and they called the council and then the council issued proceedings, so it was off to court, not once but three times, and a fine to the Lost Dogs' Home plus an apology to the kid. Jack didn't mind the letter or the fine, but the court was another matter. 'Bloody goes in circles that system,' he said afterwards, 'makes sure everyone gets paid for doing something.'

Now when there are kids about, he calls the dog close, even though it's only some kids the dog takes an interest in. He snarls at black kids with white smiles and legs that seem to go on forever. The dog also likes to chase chubby kids on bikes. When Jack sees one coming his way, he picks the dog up, tucks him under his arm. Jack doesn't have a view one way or the other about chubby kids. The same with black kids. More than once he's wondered why the footy scouts aren't recruiting them, the black kids, not the chubby kids. 'They'd be unbeatable in the back line,' he says to anyone who listens. 'Teach them to kick and you'd have a ripper of a team. Not like some of those bloody ones they recruit now days, all hairstyle. They go to water too easy.'

Jack prefers rugby but his years up and down the east coast taught him to mix it up, especially when he was down south on a job. Just now he isn't on the job on account of injury. He doesn't think he'll be back on the job either. Three years and five months since his last day at work. He reckons no one on the job misses him. Not that he really cares. He doesn't like having the pain though. Every morning he and the dog go down to the paper shop and afterwards around the park. It feels better after a walk. He knows a lot of them now, the other dog owners. There are some real trimmers, too. 'Bloody precious,' he tells one woman. 'The dogs'll sort it out. No need for all that yelling.'

The dog gets up and moves further into the sun, snout pointing south, back legs lightly crossed, fat belly not touching the deck timber. Jack gazes at him. A little dog going to be put down, drowned probably, until Jack went into the milkbar and saw *Pup free to a good home* on a note taped to the counter. It was one of the hottest days of what was already a hot year and Jack needed a drink after the long meeting about his accident. When the milkbar lady took him out to the yard he knew straight away he'd take the dog. A little mess of a thing with whopping brown eyes that looked straight into him.

When Jack picked up the dog, he felt him go stiff.

'You'll have to handle him a bit,' she said, 'he hasn't been touched a real lot.'

Jack marvelled at how you couldn't help handle him. His ears were long jersey caramel pointing to chocolate, smooth and soft, fitting snugly between index finger and thumb. His pink belly was covered in easy spots running like liquid toffee into each other. He'd put his nose down to the flesh and breathed in the pup's belly. Jack settled him onto the back seat and drove home.

It is cooling down, equinox weather. The dog moves again, back to the brick wall, belly to the sun. There isn't much for Jack to do. Sit outside and read the paper and the book from the library about knots. He's got a nice piece of cotton rope, about two metres long. He sits tying knots, the book open on the bench beside him. It says the bowline and the hay knot are probably the most useful, but the hitch for lifting round timber is the one he is tying now. He drags a length of sapling cut for firewood from the stack by the fence. He is trying to tie it like in the book. He doesn't know if he needs to lift round timber. Perhaps. He only rides a bike now so he might be able to bring a log home from the park if there's any lying round.

Jack's always liked knots. His father knew how to tie them but there was never time for Jack to learn. After his father died, he inherited the job of taking his mother a cup of tea in bed before he cycled to work. He did that every morning until he left home, and whenever he came back to visit, he did it again. It's a long time since he's made anyone a cup of tea now. He doesn't miss it. Since he's moved, there isn't the need. He used to make Jean a cup every morning and it was only a couple days before she asked him to leave that she said she liked coffee better. Jack used to drink tea. He used to drink beer. Whiskey. Port wine. Sherry sometimes. Beer mainly. That went on for years. He did some things. Really bad things. A bit like the dog, only worse. Then he stopped.

He's stopped a lot of things in his time. Funny how things start, stop, start up again.

Fifty years and here he is tying knots. And riding a bike.

He's only just starting with the dog though.

3

Going to Folkestone

Tombstone Ted, although his real name was Ian, was a tall man. He was gangly. At least he used to be gangly before ten years of marriage settled around his belly and hips, padding them out so you couldn't tell where one began and the other ended. She, his wife, still saw him as gangly and you could see how she could do this. The outline was still there, only blurred. Tombstone Ted had a small paunch, a gut really now that he was a naturalised Australian, and it stuck out from his frame, his once gangly frame, and made a rounded lump somewhere under his hand knitted but shop bought sweater. He called it a pullover. She called it a jumper. He was English, sort of, but not now. Now he was a naturalised Australian.

Tombstone Ted had married twice. His first wife died. She had cancer. His second wife didn't have cancer. She was with him here, sitting quietly on the fold up chair. Tombstone Ted's wife, his second wife, sitting quietly. Sitting before the fire.

She liked her chops burnt. She said this. She said when they're black on both sides they're ready. She liked her sausages burnt too. Tombstone Ted liked his chops and sausages burnt. They had this in common. They both liked burnt chops and sausages. And turmeric in the rice salad. The turmeric coated each rice grain yellow, an egg yolk yellow. The rice glowed in the firelight.

Tombstone Ted, although his real name was Ian, drank red wine from a beer glass. The glass was smudged from Tombstone Ted's fingers and lips. It did not stand empty for long. He liked his glass to be full to the brim with red wine. He poured red wine like it was beer and you half expected a frothy pink head to form over the claret liquid rising in the glass to leave a pink foaming track across Tombstone Ted's moustache. But it didn't. He fitted the rim of the glass beneath his moustache, beneath his front teeth and sucked the wine up into his mouth. He smiled. He smiled all the time. His front teeth escaped from his lips and left him smiling even when he didn't mean to.

She didn't drink wine. She sat before the fire in the fold up chair. You could see the flames darting on her spectacles. You'd look at her and imagine she was a devil with glowing red eyes. But of course she wasn't. She was Tombstone Ted's wife, his second wife, sitting quietly before the fire in a fold up chair.

She didn't drink strong drink. She had a glass of soft drink. She occasionally raised it to her lips and drank back a draught of the pale-yellow liquid. Whenever the glass became empty, she refilled it from the plastic bottle she had put down beside her chair. She had drunk near on half a large bottle. She and the child.

Tombstone Ted liked women. He liked talking to women. 'When I was young,' he said, 'a few of us used to drive down to Folkestone and we used to light a fire. We used to bring a bottle each,' he said. 'Two of us would drink half of the one we brought and half of the others,' he said. 'I'd take cider and if my pal took whisky,' he said, 'then you'd know you were in for a good night. We used to light a fire,' he said, 'a big fire and sit around and drink straight from the bottles.' He chuckled and the firelight danced on his teeth, his front teeth.

'When I was young I used to go down to Folkestone,' he said, 'and sit by this fire, a really big fire we'd make and drink whisky and cider. You should have seen us the next morning,' he said, 'after half a bottle of cider and half a bottle of whisky.' He sucked up some more red wine and grinned at his listeners.

'When I was young I used to go down to Folkestone,' he said, 'and drink all night. One of my pals, the one who always brought the whisky,' he said, 'bought a sheep dog, a Border Collie, and took it down to Wales. They don't have fields much in Wales,' he said 'and the dog, being a Border dog, didn't know and rounded up all the sheep from miles around. My pal had to send him back,' he said. A black and white dog, possibly a Border Collie, stood in front of Tombstone Ted and looked at the few charred chop bones remaining on the plate on his lap. Occasionally the firelight would catch the plate in its dance and skate smoothly over the grease and single yellow rice grains.

Tombstone Ted, although his real name was Ian, liked women. He liked talking to women. His wife sat quietly before the fire. She sat quietly and let the flames flicker on her spectacles. She drank up her drink. She put the glass on the arm of the fold up chair and when one of the other women picked it up to wash she said, 'I was going to have another drink.' The woman didn't put it back. She took it away to wash.

Tombstone Ted refilled his glass, his back to the fire, and said 'When I was young a few of us used to go down to Folkestone. No ladies of course,' he said, 'no ladies at all. We'd go down on motorbikes and build a big fire, pull a lot of old timber together,' he said, 'and sit around on old car tyres and drink straight from the bottle. The fire would still be going in the morning,' he said, 'but we wouldn't be.' He laughed. 'Drink. You should have seen us,' he said, 'in the morning after a night drinking straight from the bottle. I still remember that whisky,' he said, 'and how it burnt all the way down. It was alright with a bit of cider chasing it though.' He chuckled. 'And that's what I always brought. The cider. Well, it was the cheapest, wasn't it?' He looked around at the women and the firelight made his eyes shine brightly.

Tombstone Ted, although his real name was Ian, lurked around the barbecue talking eagerly to the women. His wife sat placidly on a fold up chair before the flames reddening the mudbricks and dancing on her spectacles in tiny fingers of orange and scarlet silk. She was a thin woman and wore her thick dark hair plaited into a thick dark rope down her back. Her jacket, a sensible jacket with many useful zippered pockets and side flaps in which to conceal a child's knitted hat and vinyl mittens, was khaki. This colour did not suit her. It did however match the frames of her spectacles.

She was a tall thin woman who was used to the cold. You could tell this because of her jacket, a warm waterproofed jacket that wouldn't show the grubby stains of motherhood, much less reveal the once milk engorged breasts which in their swollen state had danced in the firelight too as she suckled the child against her skin, against the cold, in the room made warm with the fire of off cuts and broken briquettes.

If she'd been asked, she would have said, 'No, I don't like the cold.' But no-one asked her this question.

4

One Conversation with my Husband

I was wearing perfume. It did not resemble the frangipani tones of the tropics. My husband was sitting across from me in our sun-filled family room. He was a tall man; some would say good looking. He was reflected in the French doors, dappled with blossom shadows. If the French doors had been open, I could have drunk in the scent, but they were closed. It is usually not warm enough to have the doors open in this town in October.

'I want to know who it was, Jilly,' he said.

I did not reply.

'Jilly, he said, 'at least tell me that.' He paused. 'Please!'

As I said, he was sitting across the room, staring at me through his reddened blue eyes. I realised I could not recall the last time he had looked at me. I mean, really looked at me. I had grown older, hair grey, lines on my face. Plain enough to see when I examined myself in the mirror. I had no idea how this had happened. Last time I recalled looking in a mirror, my eyes had been spirited and my body strong. I mean, really looked into a mirror.

I returned his stare but lacked the capacity to invest it with more than mild interest. He sat there, my husband, and I noted that he too had changed. He'd grown thicker. His ankles stuck out from the ends of his jeans. I used to call them racehorse ankles as if he was the thoroughbred, and me his proud owner. Now they appeared pudgy and blotched.

'Who was it?' A pause.

Tentative. 'Jilly?' Another pause.

Beseeching. 'Who was it?' A short pause.

No longer caring, 'Tell me! Who the fuck was it?'

I could tell you, I thought, that he was twenty-nine years old and taught me a thing or two about passion. He was, I think Norwegian, perhaps Swedish, and spoke articulate English with an accent to make your heart work hard. Every school day nuance of fjord and Viking was contained for me in that voice of his. Every story I'd ever been told about bleached wood furniture, sardine canneries and Kosta Boda glassware, popular once as wedding gifts, came back to me. Yes, he had been to Finnish Lapland, where he had feasted on great slabs of cod and reindeer steaks. He had been to Barcelona, where he wandered its stony and narrow streets at night, looking into curtained doorways where women in vaporous garments beckoned him to come in and buy cava. He had been to Baton Rouge, where he passed from pub to pub, listening to men sing the blues. He had even been to Australia, where he sang with Aborigines, or so he said. He called himself a musicologist. He was just back from the highlands where he had listened to instruments carved from stone and mahogany by men who had lived a life without seeing a white man's skin. I suppose he was intending to spend his days lecturing in conservatoriums to people who could make a piano dance under their fingers. He made me dance. He said, 'I love the way you move.' Before this I had only been to The Great Barrier Reef.

Or I could tell you, I thought, that he was fifty if he was a day, and having recently left his wife, he had come in search of something, not himself, just easy sex. He took time to talk to me about his job, his children, his wife, his favourite team. I listened, sipping my drink, sizing him up. He asked me to lunch, and we met at his hotel. It was one of those places with uniformed staff and a swimming pool, set right on the beach front, behind a low stone wall. The wall was high, but not high enough to prevent the children, who made a living selling pineapples and coconuts to sunbathers, from softly calling out and slipping over a perfectly pared pineapple in exchange for a few coins. He ordered from the side menu headed Continental and I, infatuated as I was, ordered Local. We took our coffees to his room where he produced a bottle of liqueur. We drank too much. I became garrulous and began to tell him about my life. He said, 'You are a very interesting woman, Jilly.' He reached over and put his arm around me. At first, I was quite comforted.

Or I could tell you, I thought, that he was twenty-three years old. He worked as a sometime fisherman who subsidised his earnings, taking tourists out beyond the reef, a reef not unlike The Great Barrier Reef, only smaller of course, where they could snorkel and admire the tropical fish. He spent his evenings in the bars where he might run into the folk he ferried out during the day, hoping they would buy him a drink or two. He did a good line in conversation. He could chat in several languages, scattering his talk with smiles that everyone found endearing. At first. He wore tourists' clothes, clothes they had grown tired of and given to him. His hair was tied back more often than not, and at night he took turns with other men, playing guitar and singing. He liked Bob Marley and one night he said into the microphone, 'I'd like to sing the next song for a very special person who's here tonight. She is beautiful and she is the woman in red.' He sang, looking at me and smiling. I was good for three or four drinks that night, and perhaps other things as well. He walked me home along the waterfront, small chips of phosphorescence catching in our toes as the waves lapped our bare feet. We sat for a time on the sand outside my room. He planted his mouth on mine, grabbing me in an embrace that matched the naivety of his lips. Let me show you how I like to kiss, I said, and I brushed my bottom lip against his, licking it lightly with my tongue. The following evening, I bought him a meal and he took me walking to the hot springs. He turned out to be an attentive student.

Or I could tell you, I thought, that he was forty-one, a university tutor, there like myself, on holidays. He was a small man and although I don't like small men, he had a way with words. He didn't wear a tweed sports coat with leather elbow patches, it was too hot, but I could picture it draped over the chair in his room, warming his back as he sat huddled over papers submitted for comment by surly students. I could envisage him making enemies. He could barely order a drink without it sounding like a command. He took no interest in the local sights, and as far as I knew, had not even ventured to his hotel swimming pool, let alone out beyond the reef in some precarious handmade craft. The first night we talked he watched me fixedly, drinking in my lips and eyes as if they could slake his thirst for knowledge. I found this aspect of him appealing; it had been a long time since someone had listened to me while they watched. We ordered beer and lingered into the time when dinner was more than over. We walked into the village and back again, savouring each other's company as salt starved cattle might lick from salt blocks with their long pink tongues. We kissed. Of course. Who wouldn't kiss a man who said, 'Jilly, you're a very intelligent woman,' as he put his hand on my bare shoulder.

I looked again at my husband. He sat there. Still. His blue eyes red.

No, I was not yet ready to answer him.

5

The Leaf Sweeper

The day, like others before and most probably others to follow, is still, warm, and temperate. Mrs Sonja Hadzec with her straw broom is sweeping the apron of clean black concrete outside her front door and in front of the double garage where more money than I earn in two years waits for her to jump in and drive to school to pick up the children. It's not a big trip, somewhere between eight hundred metres and a kilometre, and although the day is sunny, there's no hint of rain, and her children are athletically inclined, she prefers the drive. The need to be safe may weigh heavily upon her, or maybe the convenience of jumping in, reversing out and up the street and picking up groceries on the way, or maybe because the thing is there and it doesn't get used a lot except for shopping and the school runs, or maybe she feels different when she's in it because it's big and powerful and clean.

This day holds in store an unexpected event for Mrs Sonja Hadzec but as yet she has no inkling of what is about to occur.

She sweeps the few leaves that have drifted onto her concrete. 'They shouldn't be allowed to have all those trees,' she says to a neighbour, and to another she says, 'I don't mind the trees but I hate the leaves.' As if it might be possible to have one without the other. Mr Hadzec said he wanted to cut down his neighbours' trees and when he first purchased the land where he built the cream-rendered thirty-eight square two-storey five bedroom, three bathroom property with study, parents' retreat, laundry chute and outdoor pool, he did cut down eight or nine trees and the pair of white owls that nested in one of them must have found another home because they have not been seen since.

It took three years and five months between cutting down the owls' tree and Mr and Mrs Hadzec moving in. They pulled the ute and trailer up close to the open double garage and spent all day, and the next, carrying boxes and bags and chairs and things into the house that already had its windows draped, sheer-curtained, and blinded. The cable TV man came, then the swimming pool man, then the indoor wood heater man, and then not long after, the carpet cleaning man. I might add that this man comes every three months as regular as clockwork since moving in day. She said that a well-maintained carpet would last for years, and Mr Hadzec said he thought it was a bit too regular, but she said, 'David, it is my house and I think I should be able to care for it the way I see fit. You go to work and don't see how much opportunity there is for filth and muck to build-up. Leave it to me, David.' And so, he did.

'She's very clean, that new woman,' one of the neighbour's

says, and another says, 'I can hear her vacuum cleaner clear as a bell every day, even Sundays, so I'd be thinking she must be very dirty. All that cleaning and all that house. Just for the two of them. Seems a shame.'

It was as if Mr and Mrs Hadzec heard the local talk for the children came tumbling along, one, two, three. 'I'm not going back again,' Mrs Hadzec said before the third, 'even if it is another boy. Three it is. There's enough to do with two around the house.' Clint followed by Murray followed by Lyle. She purchased matching outfits and sent them onto the clean black concrete to drive their plastic cars and trikes and push their plastic wheelbarrows and throw their plastic balls while their father was at work on Saturday afternoons. She used the time to sweep up in the garage and fix some things in the garden bed and did not expect that one of them would get bitten by the dog next door when the child careered over the road at full tilt. She knew that Clint poked sticks in through the fence, and so did Murray, and she had overheard her neighbour telling the boys not to, as the dog doesn't like it, but she wasn't going to stop them as she didn't think much of little yappy dogs then, and thinks even less of them now.

First thing Mrs Hadzec did was ring the Council and over they came, one, two, three, tumbling out of the white SUV with the insignia on the driver's door, forms and paper and blue uniforms. They set to work posing questions and taking photographs of the road and the footpath and the neighbour's house and the dog. It went to court of course, but there was no case, as it was clear as a bell to everyone concerned that the dog had bitten Clint. A Council man even took a photograph of Clint's bottom where it was bruised on account of the bite, a thing Mrs Hadzec would normally not have tolerated as she knows that there's the possibility of more than just a picture being taken, but under this circumstance she had no misgivings. Clint pulled his elastic tops and underpants down sufficiently and the man from the Council clicked the digital and then Mrs Hadzec looked at the image and said it was okay with her if he used it in the files.

It was after all of that she took Clint to the Doctor's and then his father came home.

'It was disgusting, David. The neighbours haven't apologised or anything. It's a disgrace,' Mrs Hadzec said.

Mr Hadzec said, 'Is Clint alright?'

She said, 'And do you know his pants weren't even ripped?'

Then it was off to school again because that evening was scheduled as school concert evening and Clint's class were miming and dressing up and everyone would be there with their grandparents and video cameras and so would the Hadzecs, dog bite or no dog bite.

When the neighbour rang to enquire about Clint it went to voice message and Mrs Hadzec didn't call back. 'It's up to them,' she told her husband, 'to come and see us and apologise and ask how Clint is.' But they didn't. They rang again, that is true. Yet it left her with an empty feeling which she couldn't get rid of, and so when she heard a ruckus involving the postman years later, she stopped her sweeping and listened closely. She made a decision there and then that this would stop for good.

Although she hadn't seen a thing, Mrs Hadzec bounded

into the big, powerful and freshly cleaned car and drove after the postman, leaping out when she spotted him. She said, 'Did that dog bite you? It bit my eldest one day you know, and the neighbours didn't even say sorry. It's a pest that dog. I've been onto Council about it, and they gave me a logbook to keep about its barking and all, but is doesn't make any difference and the neighbours don't speak to me because they got in trouble when it bit Clint.'

The postman, a tall thin drink of a man with a wispish brown moustache and pale deep-set eyes listened hard, looked at his postal issue motorcycle boots, and then went to see the boss after he had completed his delivery round. He told the story of how the dog bit him and how it hurt like hell for half an hour and how there was this really nice lady next door to where it happened who could back him up and how the dog is a known biter. He wanted to know if the boss could let Council know about the attack because the community would expect that of him. He was only doing his bit to keep the community safe.

The men from the Council came back, this time in two SUVs with insignias and four men with forms and paper and blue uniforms. They took more photographs of the street and the neighbour's house and the dog. They talked to everyone who walked up and down and a few days later it was Mrs Hadzec's pleasure to invite them in for an hour or two so they could get down her story. She gave them coffee and biscuits and they seemed very nice and happy to be there. That night Mrs Hadzec said, 'David, there were four of them here and they took photographs and wrote notes, and they are going to bring me back a piece of paper to sign and that dog will go, I know it will. I feel it in my bones.'

'Sonja, what's for tea tonight? I've been working hard today.' Mr Hadzec climbed up the stairs.

'David, I'm telling you about that dog next door. David? David?'

The day of the court case Mrs Hadzec wore her emerald blouse with the lowish neckline over black wool pants and finished off her outfit with new patent low-heel boots. 'Do I look alright, David?' she asked her husband, but he was off out the door and couldn't spare more than a glance. 'He works a lot, my David,' she said to herself. Recently his times away from home stretched on from dawn until well after dusk and Saturdays were turning into Sundays and the boys spent more time on the concrete out the front yet there wasn't in truth a lot to do in the garden bed, but she believed she must be out there to keep a weather eye out for odd things.

The postman wore jeans. The Council men were in smart blue suits and carried their papers and forms and photographs in a cardboard box, there was so much of it. The solicitor came in black heels, high and thin, and pulled a wheelie suitcase. Mrs Hadzec's mother and father-in-law came along too, and as one they enjoyed the morning sitting in on a case about drink driving and another about parking and even one about littering, but not "their case", as Mrs Hadzec liked to refer to it as. When the Magistrate said that it was just a little dog that had gone a bit too far on this occasion and ordered that it go in for obedience training at the dog shelter, Mrs Hadzec's face went from white to red. Mrs Hadzec said to the other Hadzecs, 'How many more people have to be savaged before that dog gets sent to hell where it belongs. It's a disgrace. I'm disgusted.'

And there it was again today, barking at the postman as he arrives at her letterbox. 'Still barking, I see,' he says.

'Yes, it's a disgrace, Chris. It should have been sent to hell.' Mrs Hadzec and the postman have progressed in their relationship since the dog attack. She rarely misses a day without stopping awhile with him to chatter about this and that as he comes down the street on his motorcycle, pannier bags bulging with other people's letters.

'Look, there's one for you today, Sonja.' And he hands her a smallish envelope. When she looks at it, she thinks it is very like handwriting she knows. She leans the broom against the garage and turns the envelope in her fingers. She tears the seal and pulls out a single sheet and reads. *I will send more when I can. Sorry. D.* Out tumbles one, two, three hundred dollars.

The dog is quiet, but the neighbours who are inside going about their chores or hanging out their washing or tidying up their vegetable patches for winter, swear they hear it howl and howl and howl.

6 |

Ferry to Milos

She plumped down into the seat opposite, and heaved a worn backpack onto the rack that ran above the window grimed with salt spray and seagull shit. I saw from the luggage tag that her name was Sarah Robertson and her home address was somewhere in Melbourne. A tooled brown leather bag was dumped onto the floor between our legs. It sported a scene of cowboys sitting round a fire drinking from pannikins. When she settled, she left her knees apart, and I saw the crotch of her underpants, a pink slab of fabric wedged between sun-browned thighs. She was not at all like the Sarah I knew.

She pulled the bag up onto her lap and fingered its contents before taking out a pack of tissues of the sort you might buy on the way to work. She unfolded one of these and lined its edges up on the seat next to her. 'Can't bear these on for too long,' she said, tugging at the rings on her fingers. 'Makes me feel like I'm chokin'. Beginning with her left hand, she removed three rings: a large silver one studded with a cloudy green stone which no doubt came from Turkey, or maybe Thailand; a slender gold band like the one my Sarah wore; and a solitaire diamond engagement ring. This she had not worn on her ring finger, but on her pinky, where I could see it had burrowed itself in. She pulled two more from the fingers on her right hand, small red-stoned rings, garnets I guessed. She folded the tissue in and over the five rings and placed the neat package somewhere in her bag

'Mind if I smoke?' she asked, a tin already out of her shirt pocket and ringless fingers cleverly inching tobacco onto paper.

'No, go ahead,' I said.

With the cigarette lit, she leaned back into the seat and crossed one swollen ankle over the other, concealing as she did her underwear.

'Where you from then?' she asked, and I wondered if she had seen where my eyes had been. 'I'm over tryin' to get a job,' she said, 'but it's as hard here as it was at home. What's the matter with the world? Gone crazy I reckon.'

'Umm,' I said, even though I knew the world hadn't gone crazy. It was true that my world had gone crazy lately, but not the world in general. 'Jobs are hard to find for skilled people right now,' I said. I flipped open a novel bought at the airport and tried to keep my eyes fixed on the print.

'Not only hard. Bloody impossible.' She was looking directly at me. 'You got a job?'

I saw that my face was perfectly reflected in the lens of her orange-rimmed sunglasses. 'Yes.'

'Whaddya do then? Hang on, don't tell me. I'll bet you're

a teacher.' She took a long suck on the cigarette, already stained brown where she had licked the paper. 'You've got a book see, and teachers always have books.'

'You're on the money, there,' I said, and brought the book into closer focus, hoping she would see I was intent on reading and that she should stop her questions.

'I hated school,' she said. 'They say it's the best years of ya life but I couldn't wait for it to finish. Thirteen years, countin' preps, an' what's it all for? Ya get ya qualifications but ya still don't get a job.'

I pictured what it might have felt like to stand behind this long ago girl and let my nostrils fill with the smell of her unwashed hair and see the fine grimy streak on the inside of her shirt collar while I put my arm over her shoulder, perhaps nudging into her breasts, well probably nudging into her breasts as they would hang forward over the desk-top, and then I would punctuate her sentence or complete a line in her equation or do something else for her. My Sarah's breasts would not hang over desk-tops. Her breasts were small and spent their lives contained in neat brassieres.

'Oh,' I said, and I couldn't think of how I might continue or discontinue this conversation, and suddenly I wanted it to be that I'd told her that I did mind her smoking or that I'd said, *Alles ist gut in der Welt*, or that I'd leered at her crotch so that by now she would be sitting in another seat talking to someone else.

'Like this stuff.' She fossicked in her bag again and this time pulled out a notebook, its outside smothered with red and olive roses that she must have snipped from wrapping paper at some time or other and pasted onto the book's cover until the roses overlapped each other and disappeared inside the covers.

'Ah, so you're a teacher, too?' I said, and saw that I was no longer reflected in her glasses.

'Listen to this,' she said.

When you and I are together will we drive in our car down roads for hours at a time looking out side windows at cows and talk of milk prices?

When you and I are together will we stroll in furniture shops past queen-size bed sets before we ask salesmen the prices of ready-made drapes?

When you and I are together will I buy our mothers presents and sign credit slips while you sign down below 'much love' on the cards I write?

When you and I are together and we take holidays in spring will we learn to sit at restaurants without talking and look at the walls?

When you and I are together will we sleep at night for eight hours side by side in bed wearing pyjamas from our youth to keep ourselves warm?

When you and I are together would it be like this?

'I've called it When you and I are together,' she said and closed the book.

'Well,' I said, 'that was very good.' I sounded like a teacher. 'Would you let me read it for myself?' I asked.

'Ya' wanna read it? But I just read it to ya.' She handed over the book, open at the right page.

I read her lines. I counted her metre. 'I wrote it one spring. He gave me the rings, y'know, but the engagement one's too small now. I shoulda known I'd get fat. That's what me mum did when she settled down so I spose it runs in the family. Wonder what'll happen to me girl?' She laughed. 'Anyway, me name's Robby. Well, that's what me friends call me but me real name is Sarah. Sarah Robertson. I was gunna give him back his wedding ring just like I was gunna give him back his name, but then I didn't in the end. So, what's your name?'

'Stephen,' I said, 'Stephen Lampard. Pleased to meet you, Robby.'

'Well, Steve, it's nice to meet you too.' She leaned over to shake my hand as if I might be the one to employ her. 'Getting' fat. I could see it happenin' but what could I do?' she continued. 'Me mum got fat, and I bet me girl gets fat too. Course she'd die if she did, but that's what happens to the women in our family. Can't tell her nothin' though. Whaddabout the women in your family? They get fat?'

I saw Sarah standing at the stove, tongue poking at the wooden spoon I had been using to stir the evening's meal, sniffing at the contents, swallowing a bit. Then she would declare she'd had cream fettuccine, or some other rich pasta or pastry or pad Thai at lunchtime and couldn't possibly eat any dinner. She would sit at the other end of the table from me and sip a little wine while I ate. Sarah wasn't fat. Sarah had never been fat.

'Course I wasn't fat when I met him. That was a while ago, goin' on for twenty years. I was in Greece tryin' to sell shower curtains door to door.'

'Shower curtains?'

'Yeah. Is this ya' first trip to Greece then?'

'Yes,' I said, and noticed she had uncrossed her ankles.

'Well, they don't have shower curtains, didn't then and still don't today, if my last hotel was anythin' to go by. All the bathrooms end up in a terrible mess, so when I was here last, I set up a kit an' went round to hotels with me bag, which was full of curtains and rings and bathmats and stuff.'

'They don't have bathmats either?'

'Yeah, they do, sort of, but most of the places give 'em to ya as towels. Ever tried to dry yourself on a bathmat? Anyway, there I was on a Greek island, Greece is full of islands,' she added as if I might need to know this about the country I was in, 'an' I ran into him one night when I was out for tea. He was a traveller too, sold plastic tablecloth clips. Well, to cut a short story even shorter, next thing I knew we were back at his hotel, and that was it.'

Sarah took me to her room on our first date, although she never referred to it as a 'room'. *My apartment*, she had said, *is on the hill overlooking the Domain*, and as I drove, she smiled into the mirror and stroked more lipstick onto her lips. Sarah had thin lips, but she made them full by drawing a new line on her face darker than her lipstick. She always put on three coats of lipstick and kissed a tissue between applications. That night she didn't kiss a tissue. She rested her right hand on my leg as I drove to her street. The heat from her hand burned into my leg and I half expected to find a brand later, like the mark a man leaves on his cattle. She poured white wine from a cask concealed in the fridge. I looked around her room and saw a collection of hats hanging from the wall by ribbons, several black and white photographs mounted in thin black frames, a slender mirror made for reflecting mannequins, and three rubber trees in black-painted pots. She sat next to me on the sofa, and it was there that I unbuttoned her shirt, unhooked her brassiere, tasted her skin. I unzipped her skirt, and she rolled down her pantyhose. I saw that her underwear matched. It always matched. We spent the night on the sofa. Later I found this to be her bed but on that first night she did not unfold it for us. There was no time.

'Did ya like it Steve?' Robby was looking directly at me, a fresh cigarette squeezed between her second and third fingers where before the Turkish stone had been. 'Me poem. Did ya like me poem?'

My mouth opened and closed. A voice that must have been mine rushed out. 'We used to do that, window shop, and go on drives to places and stay away at weekends and eat in cafés. She began to wear pyjamas, put them on straight after work. I thought prices were what interested her because that's all she seemed to talk about but then one day she said, Stephen Lampard, I cannot bear this drivel any longer.'

I fell silent.

'We're like that too, the women in my family. Get fat and get bored. Or maybe it's the other way round.' She chuckled. 'Get bored, then fat. Either way, it amounts to the same thing.'

I took a swallow of water and felt its cool slipperiness in my throat. I looked at Robby sitting across from me, her breasts knocking against her shirt, her skirt too short, her legs tanned deep umber, her toenails painted red.

'She left me.'

'Here,' and she unscrewed the cap from a small bottle before handing it to me. 'Put some o' this in ya water. It'll make it taste better.'

I poured from one bottle to the other and watched my water turn milky white.

7

Cleaning Up

The tips of my fingers are red and tender. I have almost rubbed my fingerprints clean off with harsh chemicals, scourers and old rags. Outside the sun has warmed the concrete and I long to be on my bike with an autumn wind in my face.

The kitchen has many drawers and shelves, all melamine white; a stove top, a griller where someone grilled chops and left the fat to set on a piece of silver foil; an oven, clean, mercifully; and a Castlemaine slate floor which on account of its colour and topography does not look dirty. But it is.

The bathroom is growing two types of mould: pinkish red as well as normal blackish grey. The toilet is stained with piss and shit. There is no blood though. I washed that away before.

I heave books that no one wants to read into cardboard boxes. Ornaments, not very nice vases, some fey bookends featuring teddy bears and dolls: I pile these on the dining table to take to an opportunity shop.

It is almost eight months since my friend died. I bag her clothes and shoes and excess kitchen equipment and books about madness and astrology and drop them off at the Brotherhood. I am pleased that thirty-five size 10 women are wearing good quality moleskins and Levis, although it is possible that the same woman bought all thirty-five pairs; another five women, or boys perhaps, are sauntering the wintry streets of Melbourne in RM Williams size 5 brown or black leather elastic sided well-heeled boots.

Perhaps twenty scarves, forty hats including beanies, caps, sun visors, floppy sunhats; fifteen jumpers, many purchased at the Queen Victoria Market stall where Chinese-made acrylic yarn is woven and layered in wild parrot and ochre colours to make garments that tourists might see as symbolic of Australia; three Driza-Bones fully lined with tartan flannelette; a rust coloured sheepskin jacket circa 1976; socks, underwear, blouses; a few skirts, which struck me as very strange as the last time I saw her in a skirt would be going back to 1976 when I interviewed her for a job and she must have wanted to make a good impression. She needn't have worried. Her cow-brown American eyes and wide smile convinced me she would be just right. There were shoes in addition to the boots, including a pair of black strappy heels and numerous Nike runners; a leather jacket she had worn the first year I knew her; and so on and so forth. I don't know who is wearing those items now.

The tobacco I threw out straight away. Along with the papers and filters. It is hard to get tobacco shreds out of drawers.

In the pantry I found more than seventy cans of sardines,

in tomato sauce and au naturel; at least two dozen packets of chocolate biscuits; eight family-size blocks of chocolate; soups, stews and meals in tins too numerous to mention; and cans and cans and cans of Pepsi Max. Probably twelve dozen cans. That is a lot of Pepsi Max in anyone's language.

There was a cupboard full of flours and things ready to make Anzac biscuits, one of her favourite kitchen productions. Each Anzac Day when we went to the football, she would arrive with plastic bags full of biscuits. When she visited, she would bring several bags-full too, and I would feed kids, neighbours and myself for days on her labour. I made the biscuits this year. At half-time we sat at the MCG and passed the tin along and washed the biscuits down with a thermos of sweet milky coffee.

In the pale-green lounge room, on the brown three-seater leather couch, were the clothes she got out of before she climbed into the bath. She had also set out a clean pair of knickers and a clean bra. In her bedroom the doona was rolled back. The sheets were crisp and clean and only a light indentation proved she had been in bed, otherwise I might have thought she rolled her doona down ready to climb under on a chill August night.

Before she killed herself, she locked the dog inside with bowls of dry food, dog chews and water. I cleaned up the dog shit from the floor and picked up a book about madness that the dog had pulled from the shelves and mauled, perhaps trying to understand her close but absent owner. The dog's registration papers were left out on the table, filled in but not receipted. She was never one to pay fees unless she had to.

Dealing with a dead person's things is fraught, but it is not without fascination. There were photographs of my friend when she was four or five, dressed in a warm overcoat and sitting on Santa's knee. She was not smiling. Another picture showed her in a frilly dress holding onto her mother's hand. On either side of my friend and her mother was another girl, a little older, and a man. The sister she despised and the father she disliked.

A bible was inscribed on the occasion of her confirmation into the Catholic Church; school reports indicated a quiet and unassuming girl who achieved excellent grades; a certificate attested to the fact that she had passed her exams to become a teacher.

I found a legal paper that said she had been made a ward of the state when her mother died. Along with this paper were some notes written by my friend about her mother's death. A man, the mother's boyfriend it turned out, had come into the house, my friend let him in, and went to the lounge room where her mother sat. He shot her five times. I suppose he must have had his reasons.

What I do know for sure is that this single act was the reason why my friend took to alcohol and drugs, prescribed medicines, and alternative healing. She tried sex, work, playing cricket, bushwalking, philosophy, country living, buying stuff, joining the ALP, barracking for Collingwood, and going to AA meetings, but nothing worked in the end. In the end she took a cocktail of medicine and climbed into the bath where she tried to cut her wrist, but the cut was too small and too shallow to have any effect.

Autopsies are also fascinating. I waited and waited for my friend's autopsy report to arrive in my letterbox because I'd been told by the cop who found her that I didn't want to know how she'd killed herself.

But you see, I saw the blood, her blood, rimming the bath, more blood spots on the bathroom floor, and the pair of binoculars with the strap cut off left on the vanity. I saw a long kitchen knife on the sink, and wondered what it was doing there. I saw the drugs scattered on the coffee table. I saw the breast screen appointment on her calendar, scratched through with an angry red pen, an appointment due two days before she died.

I waited until it was summer before the postman put the buff-brown envelope into my letterbox, to discover that she had not slashed her thighs or hacked behind her knees, her flesh was not flayed and left hanging in ribbons in her frenzy to expose the cancer she was sure she had. After all, she had said to me a few days before she died, 'I've got the disease.'

I was pleased that my imagination had been more vicious than my friend's reality.

The report did confirm she had been found with a variety of scissors and knives, all of which are most likely in a plastic evidence bag at a police station gathering dust, but that the cause of death was drug toxicity. There was no cancer in her breasts, lungs or womb. Or anywhere else, for that matter.

This seems an easier way to go, slipping into a snug bath, feeling too sleepy to bother with tomorrow.

I've kept her two Pyrex measuring jugs, a glass paperweight I gave her many years ago, a copy of David Malouf's *Complete*

Stories, and a funny little silver fish, its tail twisted up as if it's jumping for an insect on a dusky summer evening.

8

Wicked Game

He will meet your eyes as you lean over the bar reaching for a beer. He will smile and you will smile back because you want to. Soon he is by your side singing the words better than the singer and then he puts down your beer, his beer, finds your hand and takes you onto the dance floor where he moves to the music holding you close to him. You dance, letting your legs and hips go with him and when the music stops, he kisses you, but you tilt your head back because you think others are watching. You will have met his wife once.

The band will play its last song and the barmaid will call for last drinks. He and you will be by the door talking and laughing and drinking and then he will say let's go. Okay, you say, and the two of you will walk out onto the street. He will say let's take it in turns to sing. You put your hands in your jacket pockets against the cold and start, your voices in harmony as you walk up the hill.

When you arrive home you will make coffee, pour brandies

and put on music. He will sit opposite talking about music, looking at you, sipping his brandy slowly. Hungry? you ask, and he says no.

After the coffee is drunk, he says come and sit over here, and you perch on the arm of his chair while he rubs a fore-finger over the instep of your right foot. Soon he will put one hand on your back and the other on your breast as he gently pushes your face down to meet his mouth. He will kiss your lips, your eyes, your neck, and you will say I don't know if this is a good idea. He will tell you he wanted you months ago when last you met. And you will kiss him back, fingering tufts of his hair as you do.

You will explore with your mouths, your fingers, your conversation. He will tell you things he doesn't tell anyone else. And you will too. You look at his eyes, the colour of Queensland butterflies. He will say don't fall in love with me. And you will look at him laughing, knowing that a bit of you already has.

Eventually you will drive him home. He will sit beside you, looking at you, touching your face. He says you must have been beautiful when you were young, and you ask does that mean I'm not now? No, he says, you're lovely. You will stop the car letting music play on while you kiss and touch and talk more. He will ask to meet for lunch, and you will say I'll be there.

You work hard during the week. On Friday you hurriedly pack your things and sign out. You walk into the cafe and see him sitting at a table smiling at you. You will be smiling and sweating and wondering why you agreed to meet him in a place where everyone knows you by your first name. You will order coffee and talk, and he will pay. He follows you home in his car. You will make ouzo on ice because it is a hot afternoon. You know you will end up making love with him even though you decided during the week not to, even though you planned what to say to him when you met. Even though you want to. After, you talk and laugh and tell him of your decision.

On Sunday morning you will be in bed reading and waiting for the phone to ring. It will. He says don't get out of bed. You will talk for hours. And then kiss. You say shh when he cries out because the neighbours might hear. You will feel silly. He will say I wasn't intending to go to bed with you this morning. You will ask why not. He will say because you are my friend.

He will come to your house the next day and you will take him to your bed. He will lay his head on your breasts while you finger his springy hair as black as crows. You will look at his eyes. Some days you will see mountains and seas in those eyes, and dull sapphires awaiting the effortless patience of the jeweller to cut them into shapes for rings to be worn on rich women's fingers.

Days will turn into weeks and weeks will turn into months. Then an afternoon arrives when you will look at the time and know you have to get up, shower, put your things in the car and drive to the airport. He will shower with you and rub soap on your back and say I love being with you. You will dry yourself quickly and put on clothes while he offers to carry your things to the car. You will kiss him in the hallway, hardly noticing him now as you are rushing to meet your plane. The fire is in your eyes. He says have a good time.

After you have flown the length of the continent you will find a place to stay and promise yourself an early night. This you will achieve because the rain hurling onto your roof blocks out the bar room music and talk. In the morning you will wake and in that moment be aware it is thirty hours since you held him.

You make your way to breakfast and think what you can do to fill in the day. You will consider sending postcards but dismiss the thought as you have nothing to write yet. You read your book and wonder if travelling suits you. You walk into the town. You spend the afternoon at the beach watching turquoise crabs climb up and down the sides of rock pools. In the evening you will order a beer from the bar and share a table with strangers. You will think about him. You will imagine his eyes fringed with black looking at you, his lips on yours, your bodies lying together. You will let your mind flip through images of him as if you are looking at photographs in an album, turning back pages here and there as you fancy. Your body will warm, and you will tell yourself to stop, knowing that of course you won't.

It is midnight in October. You will drive from the airport through the night eager to be home. You unlock the door and drop your bag. You half expect to find him in your bed. On the table there will be a big bowl of scarlet roses. Partially hidden by a dropped petal you glimpse your front door key.

9

Superman

The hut is full, every man busy reading mail or pulling off heavy boots and sweat-stained shirts before going over to the showers where the day's dirt can be sloughed off and forgotten about. Robbo sits hunched on the edge of his bed. A letter spills over the grey woollen blanket.

'Come on Robbo, you dirty bastard. Get your duds off and over to the shower. We're going out tonight remember,' yells Gary from across the room.

His bed and Robbo's are on opposite sides of the cream-painted hut, the long stretch of grey lino running like a highway between them, on down past the other seven pairs of beds all regularly covered with grey blankets and guarded by Laminex-topped bedside tables and steel grey lockers. Some of the locker doors stand open revealing insides carefully papered with magazine pictures of naked women.

'Robbo! You coming over to the showers or do we have to drag you over and scrub you 'til it hurts?' Gary asks.

Robbo glances at him. Gary is busy pulling out clean clothes from his locker and assembling them on the end of his bed along with a pile of toiletries until it looks like ten men have unwrapped Christmas presents.

'I'm not going out tonight,' he says.

'You can't pull out now, mate. We've got the big blonde chick Wendy lined up for you from the nurses' home. The one who's Sally's friend. Remember that photo Dave showed you?'

Robbo, brought up on a vast spread of farming land somewhere down the bottom left-hand corner of Western Australia with his family of brothers, wasn't prepared for photos of real girls in bikinis. National Service meant his first trip to the city with its unfamiliar ways, a pub on every corner, women wearing clothes that looked too small, too tight. When he arrived at camp and met the men it took him weeks to stop going red when they opened their lockers.

'I'm not bloody going out and that's that.' He kicks his locker door, sweeps the letter onto the floor and lunges face down onto his bed.

'What's up? Not fiancée trouble, is it?' asks Dave from the next bed along.

Robbo rouses himself briefly and looks at Dave. 'She's broken it off.' He collapses again, his dirty straw-coloured hair sticking up at the back in defiance of a visit to the barbershop a week ago. He probably hasn't washed it since, a fact that causes a deal of tension in the hut. He is one of those men who never learnt personal hygiene. Gary and Dave have spent a lot of time coaxing Robbo into learning new habits, but he is not quick on the uptake.

'What'd she say?' asks Dave.

'She said that she don't want to write to me no more and she'll send the engagement ring onto home for me. Bloody lot of good that'll do. What do I want with some second-bloody-hand engagement ring?'

'Well, that's it then,' says Gary, drawing deep on his first cigarette for the night. 'You'll have to get her out of your system. You got to get out there and find yourself another one.'

'Fuck off.'

'No, you fuck off. Me and Dave have been saying for ages she was wasn't for you. And now look what's happened. Obvious she hasn't been letting the daisies grow under her feet, that's for sure.' He takes another drag. 'After all, shelias don't break it off for no good reason.'

Robbo does not move. Gary and Dave swap looks. Wendy has been organised by the other girls to make up a six, and if Robbo doesn't turn up, she'll be like a lemon.

'Come on over to the canteen,' says Dave. 'We can have a beer and think about it.'

Robbo drags himself up from the pillow and throws his heavy legs over the side of the bed. He stands slowly. He lumbers over to the doorway and disappears through it leaving Gary and Dave to follow behind.

The canteen is set near the parade ground where every morning the men line up for inspection. One of the reasons Robbo gets away with being dirty is because of his duty, which is dunny diver and shower scrubber for Block B, therefore he regularly misses inspection. He volunteered for the job, much to the relief of the other fifteen men. It's a running gag that he spends more time than anyone in the shower block, but still stinks like a polecat.

By the time Gary and Dave get to the canteen Robbo is enthroned on a barstool gulping down a glass of whisky. A beer stands to one side. He raises it and swallows it whole.

'Ready for another one?'

'Yeah.'

'I been thinking,' says Gary, 'it's probably a good thing you're not coming with us tonight anyway. Remember last time how you wore that blue-striped suit with that hat and the girls wouldn't kick on because they reckoned you'd be mistaken for a plain clothes cop.' Gary grins at the other men standing at the bar.

'And what about that time at the ball and you came back in after cracking it with a sheila, dunno how you did, but you did, with vomit all down your front saying there must have been something off in the supper.'

Robbo lifts his head and glares at Gary. 'You're a cruel bastard.'

'Maybe so Robbo, but have a bloody look at yourself. You even wear army issue underpants. How you ever find the opening beats me cause there's enough material in a pair of one of them to make sails for the Queen Mary. Come to think of it, that's probably where they get the material from.'

'Leave off,' says Dave, tipping his head to the side. 'We're going out and that's all that matters. If Robbo wants to change his mind, all well and good, but there's no use telling him what a mess he's made in the past or that his suit is a...'

'Fuck you!' Robbo turns on his stool and sits face on to them. 'Fuck you both!' His voice is loud and the other men shift away from the bar. They've seen Robbo angry before.

'I'm sick of listening to you two. It's the same every time we go anywhere. 'Robbo, you can't wear your grandfather's trousers,' or 'Robbo, you had a shower yet?' as if I can't look after myself. Of course having a fiancée don't count,' he spits, 'even though you two can't even get a regular root cause you're too bloody busy worrying about how you look in some poncey shirt a poofta wouldn't even wear, and how you put that bloody aftershave stuff on 'til you stink to high heaven. Gives me a fucken headache, that stuff, I'm telling ya.' He stops and swills down another beer. 'Two bloody fucken experts.'

No-one speaks.

'Go on. Take me along tonight and show me how it's done if you're so fucken clever.' Robbo sits back on the stool. A thin line of spit runs down his chin from one corner of his mouth, tracing as it goes the outline of some muddy outback creek. 'Well, you gunna take me or what?'

Gary and Dave put their beer glasses on the bar and walk towards the door. Robbo hoists his body off the stool and follows.

The parade ground is dark now and they pick their path to the hut using the lighted windows of fifty buildings, as a bird might use the stars to navigate.

From the end of his bed Gary picks up a pair of low-cut jocks with a picture of Superman on the crotch. 'First things first. You're not wearing the army ration tonight. Get into some real undies.' He spins the jocks on his forefinger and twirls them across to Dave, who catches them effortlessly.

'Yeah Robbo, get into some real undies so you can get into some real undies.' Dave minces around the room, hips waggling to the beat of an imaginary rhythm, holding the pair of jocks out before him like a bullfighter holding silk.

The three men laugh out loud for the first time that evening.

Showering and dressing proceed smoothly. Robbo agrees to wear what the other men suggest and in no time they are packed into Gary's car and heading down the hill road past the Eagle and on into Adelaide. The girls show up on time and Robbo is introduced to his date. Wendy is a tall dark-eyed woman from Penola, a farmer's daughter in town for three years, living at the nurses' home.

'There aren't many beaches around Penola,' she tells Robbo when he asks if she swims much.

The three men make a time to meet back at the car before Robbo steers Wendy off in the direction of the Southern Cross where Gary has insisted Robbo take her for dinner. 'Show her you know more than just which end of a sheep is which,' he had said.

The waiter shows Wendy and Robbo to a table and returns with the wine list after making a great fuss of getting Wendy in the chair, pulling it out, pushing it in, smiling all the time. He even flicks out a starched serviette and places it on her lap.

Robbo who is left to negotiate his own chair, points to the first thing that catches his eye. 'Bring us a bottle of that.' He adds 'please', but the waiter is already on his way to the bar and doesn't hear him.

Wendy is very easy to talk to and Robbo relaxes into the evening as if they have known each other for years. Thoughts of his fiancée are far away as he leans across the table and studies the contrasting picture Wendy's dark eyes and blonde hair make against the deep red of the wallpaper. 'Enjoying yourself, love?'

Wendy treats him to one of her smiles leaving him in no doubt about the tingling sensations which are beginning to dart and scurry around his chest and belly.

'Could you just excuse me for a minute?' He pulls away from the table, looking around for the discreet sign that will point him in the right direction. His eyes focus on it and he turns to Wendy, fixing her with a grin before making his way through the crowd of tables and diners to the partially concealed doorway.

Robbo hears Dave and Gary return to the car. 'She wasn't bad tonight, great girl,' says Dave.

'A real ding-dong goer, I'd say.'

He listens as Gary strikes a match. 'Can't wait for next Saturday. Reckon we can get Robbo over the line again?'

'I reckon mate,' says Dave. 'Speaking of Robbo, wonder where the silly bastard is?'

He hears his name punctuate the night air like a bullet. He heaves himself from the crouching position he adopted between the fence and the trunk of an oak that has served as his backrest for longer than he wants to know, his legs tingling as the blood surges downward. He sees the other two standing next to the car, yellow in the glow of an overhead light. He stumbles over trying to wipe off the clinging bits of dry grass and leaves as he goes. His hair is sticking up and the front of his shirt and pants, both borrowed from Dave earlier in the evening, are patterned with muck and grime.

Dave is the first to speak. 'For Christ's sake! What've you been up to?'

'What happened?' asks Gary. 'God mate. You look a right picture.'

'Fuck off,' snarls Robbo.

The men get into the car. Robbo clambers into the back and arranges himself full length along the seat. Gary lights another cigarette and turns the key in the ignition. It isn't until they get to the Eagle that the silence is broken. Dave shifts in the passenger seat, half turns to Robbo and says, 'What happened mate?'

'Do ya really want to know?' he asks, the neon signs of the city lighting up his face with green tinges.

Gary and Dave say yes in unison.

'Everything was going real well. Wendy was talking her head off about the farm and nursin' and everythin' and the place was real nice. Then I got the urge to go. I unzipped the fly as usual and went to find the opening like I'm used to, but there wasn't any fucken opening was there? Just these stupid bloody Superman things with a bit of elastic at the top. I managed the first bit alright but then halfway through, the bloody elastic flicked out from underneath me finger and I was still right in the middle of it.'

'You mean you were still...' Gary lets the rest of his question drift away.

'Yeah.'

'What happened then?'

'What do you think fucken happened? It went all over me, didn't it?'

The two men in the front stare at the long black road snaking out ahead of them.

'I walked out the dunny door and she didn't see me, so I walked up the stairs and out into the street.'

'You mean you left her there by herself?'

'That's right.'

'No explanations, no money for the bill, no nothing?'

'I fucken left her. Superfuckenman left her.'

'You're a bastard, Robbo,' says Dave quietly.

The men drive on in silence. Well after midnight, Gary turns the car in through the heavy wooden camp gates and parks it behind Block B.

10

Ena Harkness

Peter began to love roses the day his mother cut Ena Harkness, wrapped the stems loosely in day old newspaper and said, 'Take these to school for Miss Fitzgerald.' He put his head inside the paper and inhaled the dark sweet scent. He held them carefully all the way in the car and when his mother let him out at the school gate, he barely noticed the others.

'What you got there, Pete?'

'He's got flowers!'

'Flowers?'

'Yeah, Pete's got flowers!'

Peter proceeded into the schoolroom where he laid the bunch on the front desk. 'They're lovely Peter. Are they from your mother's garden?'

'Yes Miss Fitzgerald.'

'Do you have a large garden at home?'

'Yes Miss.'

'I'd like to come and see it one day. Do you think that might be alright?'

'Yes Miss, I'll ask Mum tonight when she picks me up.'

He took a glass jar from the shelf running the length of the blackboard, went outside to the drinking taps and filled it to the brim. Remembering the stems would displace some of the water, he poured a measured trickle into the trough and brought the jar inside. Carefully he unwrapped the blooms. Picking up first one stem, then another, he set each in the jar as he had seen his mother do, although she used proper vases. Peter put his roses on the shelf in the centre of the blackboard just above the letter 'M'.

All week he sat at his desk and watched Ena Harkness. He saw the tighter buds open in the warmth and full-blown blooms drop their petals that shrank and darkened with every day. On Friday after the last lesson, he took the jar from the shelf and carried it outside where he emptied the spent blooms under the boobialla.

'Mum, can you cut me another bunch of roses for school?' he asked his mother the following Monday morning.

'Peter, we're running late as it is.'

'Please Mum.'

This time she cut him Papa Meilland and Sutters Gold. He laid them on newspaper on the table and she rolled them up, twisting the paper around the stems before slipping on a rubber band.

When school broke up for the summer holidays Peter asked his father to tell him the names of all the roses. 'Ask your mother Pete. She's the one who loves the roses. I hardly know one from another.'

On Boxing Day, she took him into the garden and told him what he wanted to know. 'This one's Lady Hamilton, Peter, she's a real beauty, flowers all the time. And over here's Buff Beauty. I love the way it climbs over the separator shed, don't you? And Guinea, my favourite red I think although it's hard to choose, what with Papa and Ena and Black Boy. They all smell lovely,' and she dipped her nose into each and every one as they walked around. There was Peace and Adolf Horstmann, Boule de Neige a tightly packed little white with soft pink outsides like a newborn lamb's ear, Nancy Hayward in the wisteria, The Reeve, Vol de Nuit, Madame Alfred Carriere and Sparrieshoop. There were more, but Peter got lost. He was tipsy with their names and their perfumes. He set about learning them by heart and by February he was able to tell Miss Fitzgerald the names of all the roses that grew in his mother's garden.

Peter moved on to secondary school and he stopped taking roses for his teachers. He told himself the long bus ride would do them no good.

Not long after he took up with Babs. She was a dark girl and drove a car as she put her age up at the police station. They got along well enough for a while, but he would be kissing her and thinking of how to repair his bike or what shirt to wear on Saturday night. He supposed Babs got wind of his thoughts because she told him it was off between them. He didn't mind, and soon found himself going out with Celie. After Celie came Joy, and after Joy came Margaret. Margaret was a different girl altogether. For a start she was older than him and had already been engaged. They walked in the garden every time she came over and Peter loved to show her the roses. 'This one needs a summer prune too, just a light one,' he said.

'You know a lot about roses, Peter. I'd like roses in my garden I think.'

'Would you?' And before he knew what he was doing he said 'We could have a big bed out the front with standards and bushes, and all along the side we'd have climbers right down to the back fence and then there'd be room for some more bushes to block off the veggies and some on the garage and on the driveway too. American Pillar. That looks good up a driveway. We could build a portico and have a rose on each column. Just think. Twenty or thirty of them. We'd be covered in roses.'

They were married in December. After a short honeymoon on the river they returned to town and set up together at the end of the main street. Peter began at once to dig the garden he'd promised Margaret, while she set about putting the house in order, sewing new curtains, setting their wedding presents in the crystal cabinet and giving the linoleum a thorough cut and polish. April came and went in a flurry of rose catalogues and July saw Peter burying over a hundred fresh rose canes in his beds. He pushed a stake into the earth in front of each one on which he affixed the labels. He meant to spend more than a few evenings tooling names onto aluminium strips and glueing them on as a permanent reminder of who his new beauties were. In September, they rewarded him with cornelian shoots that he sprayed every other morning, as a precaution against disease.

The roses grew lustily and by November the garden was dotted with colour. He did not lose a single one. 'Margaret, get out the rose bowl. I've just picked our first armful.'

'You get out the rose bowl!' She slammed the oven door so hard the egg timer fell down the back of the stove. He put his roses on the kitchen table and quietly unlocked the crystal cabinet. He set his blooms into the mesh top and gingerly poured in tepid water before dropping in an Aspro, the better to preserve them. He pushed the bowl to the centre of the table and stood back to admire his work.

'Don't leave them there. They'll drop petals all over the place.'

When their first child arrived in July, Peter had long forgiven Margaret her first outburst and indeed, the many others that followed, reasoning as he did that having a child was no easy task. He wanted to call their girl Rose, or at least Rosemary, but Margaret wouldn't hear of it and so she became known as Sharna. Peter wasn't sure he liked the name, but he loved his girl and it wasn't long before she was following him around the garden.

After Sharna came Patricia and after Patricia came Deidre. Margaret said enough was enough and moved Peter into the guest bedroom. He knocked up some bookshelves in the garage and soon felt at home with his wireless next to the bed and the rose bowl, always full, on the dresser near the doorway. Peter replaced the water every morning before work and was mindful to pick up any dropped petals, although he liked the way they layered one another like a litter of puppies.

And then a strange thing happened. Overnight all the new shoots and buds disappeared from his roses. When he went out in the morning, he was so struck he could not even bring himself to play with the girls as he usually did every morning, before they went to school. The next morning was the same, only new wood had disappeared and dark tough leaves too. That night he sat up in the chair at his open bedroom window and watched. He wasn't sure what he would discover and because his suspicions were aroused, he wasn't at all sure he wanted to discover anything.

Around eleven he saw something. He squeezed his eyes into slits and looked hard into the dark. There, down by the garage, beside American Pillar. He saw it again. It was something big. 'Oh Margaret, don't let it be you,' he moaned. 'I've tried, I really have. Leave my roses Margaret. Please leave my roses.' Margaret emerged from the dark and moved down the driveway right past where he was sitting. She was so close he could have touched her. She was carrying a suitcase. His eyes followed her until she disappeared into the black night. Almost immediately a car drove off. 'Margaret, who else is in this with you? Why are you killing my roses like this and taking them away in suitcases?' He tried to keep his eyes fixed on the garden, but his troubles had welled up so much that tears poured down his cheeks.

He sat for a long time at his window. He wondered what he would say to Margaret in the morning.

But in the morning he didn't need to say anything for he

found a note first thing on the kitchen table. Peter, there's enough cut lunches in the fridge to last the week and the girls all have clean uniforms in the wardrobe. Look after them as well as you do your roses. Margaret. He still had it in his hands when he walked around the garden, and when the girls came in for breakfast.

'Where's Mum?' Sharna asked.

'She's gone to Aunty Lizzy's for a few days.'

'Great!' squealed Deidre, 'you can drive me to school, and I can take as many roses as I like.'

He crumpled up the note then and threw it in the firebox. 'Yes, you can too my girl, you can.'

Days turned into months and the girls stopped asking about Margaret. He was relieved in a way, because he had the extra burdens of running a household to consider as well as his nightly schedule of possum trapping, for he had discovered that it was possums, not Margaret at all, that were systematically destroying his roses. He tried laying baits; he borrowed possum traps from the RSPCA and carted his quarry forty miles away; he set up electrified wires; he even bought a shotgun and sprayed possum innards over the garden. But still they came every night and ate any tender young growth they could find. Peter began to think of it as a war, and knew in his heart when over seventy of his beauties were eaten beyond regeneration, that it was a war he was losing.

One evening, just on nightfall, he and the girls walked home through the gardens in town after the pictures. They saw a young possum crouched low down in the hollow of a tree. The girls stopped.

'Look at its eyes, Dad. They're pink, just like its ears.'

'Yes, Dee they are. And can you smell that scent of fear about it?'

The girls sniffed, looking a bit like possums themselves, he thought, and yes, they could all detect a muskiness, quite different from anything they had smelt before.

'Have we still got possums in the garden Dad?' Sharna asked, 'because if we have, I want one for a pet.'

When Peter looked again at the animal, its eyes big and its whiskers trembling, he could not find it in his heart any longer to muster up the hatred that had kept him going for the eighteen long months of possum warfare. He returned the traps, dismantled the electric wires, and sold the gun to a dealer. He found he had more time to spend with the girls and they went on picnics to the hills.

Peter read up a bit about possums and began to lay crumbled bread and birdseed along the kitchen window ledge. He put out bits of quartered apple too, and within a month four possums were regular feeders. Peter started to leave the window open and talk quietly to the possums as they fed. One night he reached out his hand and stroked the black-tipped fur running along the back of the smallest possum. It hardly flinched. 'Come on my beauty,' he cooed, 'come to Daddy, come on, come to Daddy.'

Before long the possum would leave the window ledge and climb along Peter's outstretched arm settling down on his shoulder. He would bring round his other arm and pat her, for he was sure she was female being so small and so daintily coloured, at first quite lightly and rhythmically as if she were a cat. Soon he was able to shift the possum with his hands and hold her cradled in his arms, making it easier for him to stroke her.

Peter's interest in possums grew as did his possum collection. He gathered about him some thirty of the creatures before twelve months was out, many of which became regular visitors in the kitchen. The girls were enthralled.

When Sharna went to the big secondary school, she asked Peter if she could bring a friend home to see the possums. 'Of course, love,' he said, 'everyone's welcome here, even the possums.'

Sharna's friend Anne walked into the kitchen. 'Where's your mum?'

'She's gone to Aunty Lizzy's.'

'When will she be back?'

'Dunno.'

'When did she go? This morning?'

'No, almost three years ago now.'

'Three years! What's she do there?'

'Dunno,' replied Sharna, who hadn't thought about Margaret for some time, and in all truth didn't know what her mother did.

'My mum wouldn't have let me come if she'd known that. Anyway, what are all these for?' Anne pointed to some two dozen brightly coloured bowls lined up on window ledges.

'They're for Dad's possums.'

'Your dad's got possums?'

'Yeah. They come to feed every night.'

'Where?'

'Here. In the kitchen.'

'In the kitchen? Boy, no one lets possums in their kitchen. My dad reckons they're vermin.'

By next Monday recess Sharna found herself in the centre of a ring of girls in the schoolyard. 'Sharna's a possum lover. Sharna loves possums. What do ya do with the possums Sharna?' shouted the girls. Anne shouted loudest of all.

That night Peter put his arm around Sharna as he could see that something was up, but she shrugged him off. 'I'm sick of these bloody possums!' she shouted. 'There's never any Rice Bubbles left for us in the morning. And when's Mum coming home?'

Peter didn't know what to say so he said nothing at all. Instead, he began filling the bowls with all the possums' favourites: wheat germ, apple, sunflower seed, Rice Bubbles. 'Well, my little beauties, you'll have a lovely feast tonight,' and he smiled at his reflection in the kitchen window.

He opened the window and sat down at the table. 'Come on, come to Daddy,' he crooned as the first possums appeared out of the dusk. Peter looked out for his special possum, the little female that first allowed him to get close. There she was, perched over on the fence. 'Come on baby, make your little Daddy happy tonight,' he whispered, as she clambered down and made her way up onto the window ledge. She quickly settled down into the crook of his arm and he began stroking her, gradually increasing the pressure of his hand, all the while murmuring close to her pink ears. As he had come to expect, she raised her thick muscular tail and brushed it over his face, emitting as she did a sweet dark odour, not dissimilar Peter thought, to Ena Harkness.

11

Too High for Comfort

You'll think I'm making this story up, but I cross my heart and hope to die that the last words he said before he left were I love you Angela, but I can't live with you anymore. Of course I didn't believe him. Would you? He'd been telling me for years how much he loved me. I hadn't asked to be put on a pedestal, mind you, and of course I wouldn't be honest if I didn't admit to having liked it for a while. Here's a man after all, one of those mortals our mothers warned us against because of their potential to leave us with child in any number of circumstances, axe murder us, and or run up huge debts with our money, at first treating me like I was a new invention, indeed one that can solve most of the world's problems, probably even starvation and the refugee crisis, but especially solve his problems. And that's where the catch is. It's all very well to be perched on a pedestal receiving passionate tongue kisses, but I found all this receiving became a bit tiresome, and besides, I began to suspect that he could see right up my nose.

I asked him about his ex. This led me to one of my finest observations about pedestals. The larger the ghost of last year's ex, I use this phrase loosely, the higher the pedestal. After all, if one woman has crashed down around his feet, he might work to guard against such a thing happening again.

But I digress. Back to the ex. I asked him a range of personal questions, like what did sleeping together encompass; did she do what I did; did he once like what she did; did he still like what she did; what colour her underwear was; and could she cook falafel. This last question must be seen in context, as you see he took me out to a Lebanese restaurant and pronounced falafels to be the best thing he'd ever tasted and after I paid the bill. Always on the alert for ways to please, given that I was not yet last year's ex, I went home and cooked up a huge Middle Eastern banquet: falafels, babghannouj, kibbi, tabouleh, flat bread, ma'amoul.

On reflection he failed to answer most of these questions satisfactorily. Not even the undies one. He claimed he couldn't remember. This sent a clear message to me that I may as well stop wasting money on frothy bits of lingerie and return to sturdy cotton briefs that could unhesitatingly go into the automatic washing machine on full cycle without fear of losing a leg band. To give him his due he did cope well with number five. No, she couldn't cook falafel, and what's more, he doubted if she even knew what falafels were. I hadn't asked him the follow-on question. He volunteered the information himself. He looked at me and sighed with a look in his eye which I plumbed to be real pathos.

And then we got on to the child. Now you may be

horrified to hear me say that I was jealous of his child, but I was. It's hard to imagine being consumed by a furious rage when you stumble across your lover blowing raspberries on the belly of his five-year old as he dries her off after a bath, but that's what I felt. And I felt it again and again.

He didn't push me on the swing. He didn't put me in the bath and soap me all over. He didn't mash my vegetables together. He didn't dress me. He didn't tell me I was the most beautiful girl in the world. He didn't talk nonsense to me. He didn't carry me around on his shoulders. He didn't buy me chocolate frogs. He didn't stop whatever he was doing to dry my eyes if I should happen to cry. And most of the time, I made sure I didn't.

A certain restraint began to be evident. He said more cautiously Oh god Angela, I love you, with no smile at all. Just this look a well-trained dog get when its owner, who's holding the opened can of dogfood, makes it sit over near the door, metres away from its bowl.

Questions led to further questions, and even to some nasty scenes once or twice. I suspect any man can be suitably cowed by questions concerning his ex, but not so with questions concerning his child. He didn't like these questions one little bit. I didn't like them myself. But they kept tumbling out. He reacted rather strongly. I don't think I'm being over dramatic in saying this. For instance, when I asked him why it took so long to read a bedtime story and tuck his daughter in, it had taken him thirteen minutes, I'd timed him, he became a bit irrational and told me I was a goddamn fucking paranoid bitch. I didn't much like being sworn at, and one of those nasty scenes I alluded to before followed, but I won't elaborate any further right now.

As time wore on, I discovered more subtle ways of expressing my jealousy. I discovered I could dress his daughter in outlandishly ugly clothing, all the while demurring as to whether pink, her favourite colour, was suitable. Or I could fervently prepare a solid plain meal. I called such meals 'nutritious' and in serving the small being huge country helpings I'd mention the need for her to eat up all the first course before she could be served the exotic feather-light chocolate creation I'd fetchingly arranged at her eye level on the dresser. Or I could scold her for leaving the bathroom floor sodden. After all, she might slip. Or for not cleaning her teeth. Such carelessness might cost mummy money. I could do this while righteously maintaining I had the child's interests at heart. Such fine cunning was hard to play with and luckily for me she only visited every other week. I had time to rest up between bouts.

Perhaps it's appropriate at this point to share with you some of my religious views, as I know the more perspicacious amongst you will have already thought about god's women in relation to this tale. My religious education, although extensive, was in the main ineffective. I grasped at names such as Shadrack, Meshack and Abednego, names I could roll around in my mouth, and the story of Moses in the bulrushes captured a sliver of my heart. Beyond this though, and the fact that whenever I swore and looked at the altar candles, they would burn higher and smoke profusely, I remained ignorant. Mary the virgin, Madonna, Lot's wife, Delilah were names which only became illuminated much later in my life, and sadly I now think, without any of the traditional meaning which were their due. I did however grasp the significance of Eve's story. In its poignancy and grief, it is illustrative of the inherent dangers for women in being seen in roles which on the one hand don't allow for much exploration and experimentation with the world, but on the other condemn them for not fully coming to grips with temptations - now there's a biblical word - which might come their way. And of course that's what temptations do, they come from this way or that way, and the ill-equipped can do little else but succumb, as she has no guile in her armoury to resist.

Years later a Baci chocolate wrapper revealed this mystery of temptation to me more fully. The words, Oscar Wilde's words actually, were if I remember correctly, the only way to get rid of temptation is to yield to it. This was also printed in Italian and French, presumably for the edification of other foreign nationals who enjoy Baci confections. But I think these words of Oscar's reveal a certain depth of understanding about what it is to be a second wife. Yes, he knew a thing or two did Oscar. And I was beginning to learn.

After family matters came money, then friends, then common interests and then that nebulous albatross which hangs around the necks of every couple which I will loosely term 'domestic arrangements'. I'm sure you will be able to sketch in the background of how money, friends and common interests can easily become battlegrounds where one moral high ground is pitted against the moral high ground of the other, and so I won't go into these in more detail. After all it's fair to expect you to do some of the work in this story too. But I will open the door a little on domestic arrangements.

By domestic arrangements I refer to the grab-bag of items which includes who serves the drinks at the dinner party, who takes the rubbish out when both have the flu, who writes the Christmas and birthday cards, who gets the glass of water at 2.17 a.m. when both know they will still be hungover at morning alarm time, who complains first when both have been tongue kissing party guests goodbye, who goes to the supermarket and who pays (but that's touching on money matters and I don't want to go into that), who is the wittiest during a weekend away with friends at a beach house, who makes the better pumpkin soup, who chooses the colour to re-paint the study, who initiates close physical contact, who captures the huntsman from the bedroom ceiling, who phones to cancel the newspaper delivery, who drives home at night after a particularly dreary evening, who serves the most double faults in the tennis final. I could go on, but this list I think should suffice in giving you an insight into domestic arrangements, such as they are, or in my case, such as they were.

Finally, and no amount of saying, but I love you Angela, could change anything between us. And that gets me back to where I began. He left, but you already know this because it is implied early on in the story, and as he left, he said I love you Angela, but I can't live with you any longer. You know this too because I'm beginning to repeat myself, but what he really meant, what I didn't say before, was you're a nasty girl Angela. I loved you once. But in the end, you turned out like the other one. I'm leaving. And he did.

This morning, I woke early. I watched as the dawn light changed from creamy yellow to grey. I got up, donned my dressing gown and sheepskin slippers, the ones he had given me, and walked into the kitchen. The light was on in my neighbours' kitchen. I could see him standing behind her, arms draped over her shoulders, gently kneading her breasts. He was nuzzling her neck, and she was trying to fill a kettle. Her mouth was open, her head was thrown back. I could almost hear the laughter. I suppose she sat the kettle on the bench before they disappeared from view.

12

Lunch with Nettie

When I'm alone, and I'm almost always alone now, I like to have my phone in the bedroom so that if any marauders attack in the middle of the night I can quickly hit the emergency code and gasp a frightened call for help to my neighbours.

My neighbours don't know I do this, and as they are elderly would perhaps not wake to the sound of my ringing. I don't even know where their phone is in relation to their bedroom. I know it's not mobile like mine. Perhaps it is two rooms away and they are the sort of people who put on dressing gowns and slippers whenever they get out of bed, and by doing this, should I ring, the time elapsed would allow the marauder to successfully attack whilst their phone feebly rang out into the night. Perhaps they take sleeping pills. Or other pills which ensure an uninterrupted sleep. Perhaps they wear hearing aids which they take out at night. Perhaps they unplug the phone. All these variables that I have no idea about, and yet I have nominated them as my first line of life support in the event of an emergency.

Today I am not alone, however. Nor was I yesterday. Today I am at the beach. The seaside more precisely, as from where I sit in a restaurant beside Nettie, my immediate view is that of the river, and beyond that, the harbour. Thick planks form a boardwalk looking like so many rows of plain knitting. My eyes travel down the boardwalk to the bridge, beyond which must be the harbour proper I suppose, tucked over there in the murkish green grey, insipid blue, the industrial fumes of brown. I'm glad I don't have to work there. The bridge is arched to span the water. I wonder if swallows nest under those arches. And whether those hollow bodies of insects long gone cling to the undersides of the curves like they did under the pier at the lake. I hated those things, ghostly reminders of something I knew I was scared of.

People normally use a bridge to get from one side of a waterway to another, and this bridge would be no different, else it would be purposeless. But there is something hulking on this bridge. I can't seem to make it out. Is it moving towards us? Or going the other way?

The couple sitting next to us have been joined by others. They talk loudly, and I am drawn to their conversation.

'I wouldn't go on a two hour walk without the proper gear.'

'Like walking boots and stuff?'

'I mean the weather can change so suddenly.'

'You hear about all those bushwalkers who get lost. They go out and something happens.'

'And they have to send in the search and rescue squads.'

'Right. You go to any of the places, and they've got these signs up everywhere. Short walk, one hour. Now that's not a short walk. Ten, maybe fifteen minutes, is a short walk. I'd call an hour a moderate walk.'

I look over at them. Fleshy young men with their too thin wives. Two get up to go outside where I see them lighting cigarettes.

'And at night it's real scary.'

I know night is scary. When I was young, I would hear foxes howling in the distance, and fear would walk in through the bedroom door and settle like the scrapings of burnt toast on a stainless-steel sink. I hated that fear. Cold and black. That's the power a fox has over me.

I wonder if these people know that walking is good.

'Nettie, did you know that one foot contains more than a quarter of the body's bones?'

'It can't do dear. That leaves less than half in the rest of the body, assuming of course we've got two feet.' She giggled.

'True,' I pause. 'I bought a pair of shoes the other day and there was this magazine thing in the box, *The Foot Book,* or something.'

'Nice?'

'What, the book?'

She raises one eyebrow.

'Oh yeah, the shoes are nice. Just plain, but nice. And the book said that about the bones, and the sweat glands too.' Apparently on the sole of just one foot are located some quarter of a million sweat glands. These glands produce an alarming measure of sweat, amounting to a total of about one hundred litres a year for a pair of feet. I tell Nettie this.

'Incredible,' she says, and continues to knife butter onto her cut roll, smoothing it out right to the edges.

I look at Netttie. Her eyes water which makes her look like the old woman she is. From a distance, say across a dining table, it's hard to notice the damp marks under her eyes because she keeps herself well made up with compressed powder and lipstick. She prefers muted colours such as fawn and taupe, camel and cream. A small print scarf helps to keep her neck warm in winter, and she has it on now, tucked neatly into the collar of her blouse. She wears matching shoes and carries a handbag. Usually brown. Sometimes navy, sometimes black. Brown, she says, is more versatile.

After our first course, she pats her hair neatly into place, puts on another layer of Coral Blush lipstick. Pink without being too pink. A pink brown. She has no use for other cosmetics. She showed me once the collection she has amassed in the bathroom cabinet, put there after those daunting family occasions of Christmases and birthdays. Twice a year she cooks, she loves to cook, and in return is presented with talcum powder and skin perfume and scent and cologne and palettes of coloured eye shadows and small bottles of varnish for her nails. Many happy returns, they say to her as they hand over the shop-wrapped gifts, gifts covered with thick heavy foils and raffia of many colours. She wishes the paper was big enough to wrap around one of the sheaths she makes from the flowers in her garden, but it never is.

Cooks, professional cooks I mean, have told her she has

talent. Her idea had been to leave school and go to college to do a cookery course. 'Family's needs came first, though,' she told me. 'Meals had to be cooked at home three times a day when mother became sick, and none of the boys married as yet.' Ingredients were the one bit of magic she could wield as she turned lists in recipe books into appetising dishes set before them on the table. And she loved it. 'Cleans my soul,' she said to me, although she probably meant it lifted her spirits. Up from the table as soon as the family finished, she would be ready to pounce on the grubbied gravied plates and replace them with some miraculous pudding wobbling seductively in its dish. After the meal was over, she would wipe the dishes and tidy the kitchen before settling down for a quiet knit and a look at the television.

Her sleeve brushed an unused pat of butter on her side plate as she spooned the soup towards her mouth. She dabbed at it with her napkin. 'Reminds me of a blue dress I had. What clothes we wore then. We were like stuffed toys wrapped in layers and layers of dress-ups. Sleeves to drape in things. Stupid clothes really. Especially for busy people. And I was a busy person. This dress was blue, a blue like blue skies, blue eyes, blue ink. It was shot silk, I think. It changed colour with the light.'

A car backfires in the street. The sound is like gunshot. It rings out into the air. I can't tell the difference between gunshot and exhaust noise. My chair isn't comfortable, it is too low and not well shaped. Soon I'll have that hot pain dancing up and down my back, and my shoulders, already feeling as if they are draped by a concrete shawl, will grow colder and stiffer.

'I remember sitting at the table,' she said, 'while mother used the vegetable knife to take small sections of paint from the ends of my coloured pencil set. She pared them, all twelve of them, my long Colourtone coloured pencils until they looked like the canoe tree out by the lake. And then she wrote my name in block letters on each one. JAN.'

I shifted my gaze from the bridge and looked at her. 'My name is really Janet,' she said, 'and for a long while now I've gone by the name of Nettie, but when I was younger my family called me Jan. Anyway, when she finished, I put them in my pencil case. One of those with a sliding lid decorated with transfers of jolly children sitting amongst flowers. I took my pencil case to school and put it in my desk. And every day I used my pencils to complete one or other of the tasks set by Miss Kerr, who was terribly beautiful. It was 1957 when I was in Grade One and all was well with the world. I had just seen the Russian sputnik travel overhead with the dog on board. Poor dog. Eight days in space, then no more. They hadn't perfected re-entry.'

She rearranged her cutlery when the main course arrived and began to slice the roast meat into bite-sized pieces. She placed a piece on the end of her fork before stabbing at pieces of roast potato and pumpkin. 'I've never told anyone this. But one day in class I dropped a pencil, the navy blue one out of the set, and Ian Davies picked it up and put it in his pencil case. He sat across the aisle from me, and I saw him do it. I waited until lunchtime and asked him for it back. He wouldn't give it to me. He just called me names and said it was his. I asked him again and I remember he ran down the steps from the vestibule into the playground laughing all the way.' She took a sip of water. 'I decided I'd retrieve my pencil. I marched into the classroom and raised the lid of his desk. I opened his pencil case and there was my pencil with JAN etched into the bare wood. I took it. I walked out of the room. Judy Williamson and Robert Carberry, both in Grade Two, ran up the steps to where I was. Robert snatched the pencil from my hand. Ian was standing behind them, grinning at me.'

'Why did you steal Ian's pencil?' asked Judy.

'I didn't. It's got my name on it.'

'Show me!'

Robert held up the pencil and I pointed to the letters spelling JAN.

'That's not JAN,' he said, 'that's IAN. You've stolen his pencil. You're a thief.'

'All lunchtime they bailed me up there in the cloakroom corner telling me over and over again I was a thief. And sure enough the J for JAN had been transformed to an I for IAN, I could see it clearly, but it was my pencil. Ian had added the extra bar to the bottom right of the J. He must have. But Judy and Robert wouldn't hear of it. This just added fuel to their fire, and I became a liar as well as a thief.'

I glance out the window again. The activity on the bridge moves into sharper focus. Something is coming towards us. It looks like a war memorial, one of those ones where a man is perched on a plinth, slouch hat angled towards the sky, rifle over a shoulder. It is crabbing slowly across from the east to the west, carried on the tray of some heavy transport.

13

Angel Skin

Try as she might Marlene Gilmore could not get out of her wedding dress. She remembered taking it off without difficulty during the fittings before she was married to Ian, but after the ceremony and the reception when she climbed the hotel's stairs, her new husband on her arm, to change for their going away together, she found she could not budge the angel skin frock in any direction.

She undid the thirteen-inch zipper that ran from under her left armpit to her hip and swivelled the dress on her waistline before trying to lift it up and over her arms in the way her mother had taught her.

'Never step out of a dress Marlene dear,' her mother said, 'because you might catch it with one of your heels. Before you know it a whole panel of lace can be ruined.'

Marlene didn't particularly like this method, recalling as it did images of her father skinning rabbits; however, she acknowledged its good sense.

Ian tried to help by lifting the skirt made heavy with clusters of hand-sewn pearl drops and a lining of taffeta and tulle. She tried to slide one arm out from its sleeve and although the dress had a sweetheart neckline, she could reveal no more than half a bicep of bare arm. She tried with her other arm but if anything, that was worse. There was no possibility of rolling the bodice down over her chest and inching the frock over her wedding slimmed hips.

Marlene and Ian, aware of time passing and anxious to be on their way if only because neither wished to delay their guests longer than necessary, knew at last they must call for assistance. Marlene didn't like to rely on her mother so early in her marriage but what could the couple do? Ian picked up the telephone and dialled reception, carefully checking the number on the card as he did.

'Ah yes...Gilmore here...Ian Gilmore...room 303...we've run into a spot of bother...no, nothing serious...I wonder if you'd mind...I'm sorry to have to ask...could you ask Marlene's mum...Mrs Lindsay, Mrs Reg Lindsay...'

'She's the one in the mauve,' hissed Marlene.

'She's the one in the mauve,' repeated Ian, 'and tell her to come to our room...room 303...thank you...yes, yes, I will...thank you.'

Marlene's mother arrived promptly outside their door and knocked loudly before turning the doorknob. 'Oh Marlene,' she gasped, 'whatever is the matter?'

'Mum, I can't get out of my dress.' And because the strain had been so much and she was tired and wanted to get away with Ian as quickly as possible and the appearance of her mother in the room seemed such a defeat, she burst into tears standing just as she was with her zip undone and one bared shoulder hoiking the sweetheart neckline completely out of kilter.

Having already married another daughter, Marlene's mother knew better than to offer more than a passing *there, there dear* to her daughter. That was Ian's job now, and she wouldn't take it from him even though she dearly longed to encircle her pretty little girl Marlene, her daughter, her youngest daughter, her last baby after the two boys, with her strong mother's arms and rock her soothingly against her lace inlay. Instead, she said, 'Stand still dear and Ian and I will have you out of this in no time at all.'

But they didn't.

Marlene's eldest sister, the matron of honour, was sent for, but she could not move the frock. The three bridesmaids, Marlene's friends from the tennis club, made their way up the stairs and into the room which was now so full of tulle that it was hard to tell where one skirt ended and another began. Marlene looked over at Ian who was lost in the sea of blue and cream. Despite herself she found a little smile to lighten her despair. Ian picked up her cue immediately and for the first time in his married life made a decision for both of them, something he was to do many times in the ensuing years.

'Girls and Mrs Lindsay,' he said.

'Ian, do call me Mum, there's a dear.'

'Alright then. Girls and Mum. I don't think there's anything any of us can do that we haven't done already.' Jill the second bridesmaid giggled. 'I suggest Marlene and I go down and go away like we are.'

'But it's such a pity to waste the going away frock Ian,' said Marlene's mother who particularly liked the turquoise shantung ensemble Marlene had chosen.

'It won't be wasted Mrs Lind...Mum, I can assure you,' said Ian. 'She can wear it tomorrow when we go out for dinner.'

'Yes, I can too,' said Marlene, and so began the clearing of the room as Marlene's mother, her eldest sister and her three tennis club friends made their way down the stairs looking resolutely bright and eager to let the guests who were now milling around in the hallway at the bottom of the staircase know that nothing untoward had occurred.

Marlene took a couple of minutes to adjust her frock and apply a touch of powder and lipstick before she and Ian opened the door of room 303 and walked arm in arm down to their assembled guests. Confetti flew in the air hovering momentarily like lawn sprinkler drops caught in a sunbeam, before falling softly on the newlyweds. People called out and wished them well as they made their way across the hall and out onto the steps where Ian's car stood waiting. They climbed in and drove off. Marlene put her hand on Ian's left thigh.

But Marlene did not wear her striking turquoise ensemble the next evening, nor indeed did she wear it on any evening of their honeymoon. Her wedding frock remained firmly in place. She and Ian quickly learnt to work around it. People they met in the street looked at them it is true, but neither

Marlene nor Ian minded as they were in love and had each other.

Years passed and still Marlene wore her wedding frock. It became a part of her, and she grew accustomed to moving around her home in such a way as to not knock things off the coffee table. Every other day she washed herself carefully, reaching down into the bodice and up under her full skirts. Ian helped by sponging away any grubby spots that appeared on the back of the frock. This if anything brought them closer together and Marlene liked the way Ian would slide his fingers down over her shoulder and into the sleeve feeling for the ends of the damp flannel which she had slipped up her arm beginning at the wrist.

She shopped and cooked and laundered and gardened in her frock. She went visiting and to church and even played tennis for a while but gave it up after tripping on the beaded hem when going for a low drop volley just near the service line. She did not want to ruin the frock even though she still had the turquoise shantung to look forward to. She went to family birthday celebrations, visited her sisters when they had their new babies and attended every funeral she ought. Sometimes she felt a little incongruous when looking at the snaps her father took but she always cheered up when Ian nudged her and said, 'You still look as beautiful as you did on our wedding day.'

And there was no denying it, she did.

From time to time, she attempted to get out of her frock, and although it was fluid enough to allow her three pregnancies and two births, she could not remove it. Her doctor offered to snip the stitches with a scalpel on the birth of her first, but she said, 'No Doctor Watersmith. I wore it on my wedding day, and I have not taken it off since. I think it would be untimely to remove it now, especially as Ian isn't here.'

He duly complied and merely asked the nursing staff to be very careful and bring more towels, which of course they did willingly.

'It is angel skin isn't it Mrs Gilmore?' asked the midwife between contractions.

'Yes, cream angel skin Sister, cream angel skin with a taffeta and tulle underlay.'

And throughout her labour Marlene chanted 'angel skin' to herself, 'angel skin with a taffeta and tulle underlay'.

Marlene found feeding difficult at first but by undoing her zip to the waist and easing the frock sideways she was able to offer both breasts to her suckling infants without undue stress or delay. Her children thrived.

On her daughter Wendy's wedding day, Marlene again tried to get out of her frock and even though she and Ian spent a good hour together pushing and pulling, they failed. Marlene suspected Ian did not have his heart in it and neither did she really, but it was unthinkable she might spoil Wendy's day by being both a bride and the bride's mother. Wendy assured her mother she did not mind and so Marlene and Ian sat in the front left pew holding hands and smiling happily as Wendy and her groom exchanged vows. As a concession to the occasion Marlene did not wear her veil, despite feeling a trifle underdressed without it.

The unguents and creams Marlene applied to her neck and face grew thicker and richer in consistency over time to waylay as far as possible the inevitable spread of wrinkles. She changed to a slightly darker shade of lipstick to offset the greying of her once brunette hair. But steadfastly she refused to do what all her friends had been doing for years with the assistance of their hairdressers. She would not colour her hair.

'But Mum,' said Wendy as tactfully as she knew how, 'the cream of your angel skin frock isn't the colour that most suits you now, even though you still look very pretty of course. I really think you should darken your hair just a little. Don't you?'

'Oh Wendy, I don't know,' said Marlene, and she went home that evening to discuss the matter with Ian.

'Well dear, if you think it would be for the best, I'll do it,' she said after they sat side by side and looked through the family albums beginning naturally with their wedding album. At half-past eight, Marlene made a cup of tea. 'I'll ring Bettina first thing in the morning and make an appointment.' She toyed with her teaspoon and sent it tumbling to the floor. She looked at Ian, but he didn't seem to notice.

Bettina's salon was a busy place and unless Marlene asked especially for Bettina, she was likely to get any of the girls and some she hardly knew. She knew their names of course - Salina, Jan, Claire, Robyn, Rhonda, Denise - but she didn't feel at ease chatting to them as she did to Bettina who had trimmed her hair for years. Fortunately, Bettina was free at ten-fifteen and Marlene settled comfortably over the sink feeling Bettina's sudsy fingers run through her hair, cleaning down every strand in preparation for the application of the dye. Marlene recalled watching Rhonda apply a coppery paste to another customer's hair on the previous occasion she had visited the salon and knew, therefore, what to expect when Bettina assembled her tools on a trolley wheeled in from the back room. Slowly lifting each lock, Bettina painted it both sides before draping it carefully over Marlene's crown.

At lunchtime Marlene emerged from the salon brunette, her hair coloured and dried to perfection. She hurried home eagerly to await Ian, and just as she expected he turned his key in the lock at five twenty-two.

'Oh Marlene, you look just like you did on our wedding day.'

Smiling and blushing ever so slightly, Marlene set about laying their meal on the table set in advance with their wedding candelabras and a small bouquet of forget-me-nots.

The only trouble with hair dye Marlene discovered was the need to repeat the process every few weeks if greying roots were to be avoided. And so, she became a regular at Bettina's.

Bettina was no different from any other salon owner and it wasn't long before she quietly demurred that Marlene might be interested in eyelash tinting and certain depilatory procedures, especially of the facial area. Marlene understood that someone with Bettina's business acumen was not purely enticing her to spend more money, but indeed had her clients' happiness and well-being at heart.

Before long Marlene was undergoing regular colouring, tinting, manicuring, steam cleaning and hair removal from all sorts of places on her body, even those which rarely saw the daylight. Marlene marvelled at both her new-found needs and why she had not bothered to satisfy them before. She could feel her horizons expanding every time she stepped over Bettina's threshold.

After her treatments she would wait for Ian to return home, for Ian always came home promptly, and match with his comments the extent of change freshly crafted by Bettina. However, Marlene began to wonder if Ian had it in him to meet such a challenge as he invariably said, 'Oh Marlene, you look just as you did on our wedding day.'

Consequently, she decided on a plan, although at the time she wondered if it wasn't a little bit silly.

Her plan was to colour herself like she had never been coloured before. Some of the magazines in Bettina's showed how she might achieve her plan by crimsoning her nails, making her lips magenta, and even wearing her hair acid green or heliotrope, if she chose.

'Marlene, are you sure you want to go ahead with this?' Bettina asked one particular morning when Marlene pointed to the violet and cornelian striped hair of a magazine model.

'Of course, Bettina, of course.'

Marlene now thought colour was so much fun, especially stuck as she had been for a married lifetime in cream angelskin.

She began to spend her days leafing through magazines to find novel and vivacious shades with which to colour herself. More often Ian's key would turn in the lock before she laid the table.

'Marlene, my bride, I'm home,' he would call.

'Oh Ian, already.' And she would rush into the kitchen and pull pots and pans from the cupboards and utensils from the drawers. She forgot all about the candelabra on the sideboard.

One day she happened on a model sporting turquoise hair. She took the magazine to her wardrobe and yes, the colour perfectly matched that of her going away outfit. At that moment she knew she must have turquoise hair.

Ten-fifteen sharp she explained her new colour plans to Bettina who, now accustomed to Marlene's bird of paradise desires, quickly mixed the required shade, and began her preparations. Marlene watched for some time until her attention was side-tracked by the arrival of morning coffee and biscuits, so kindly delivered by Claire. In the time it took Marlene to bite off a sliver of shortbread, Bettina dropped the bowl of dye. It fell onto Marlene. The dye ran over her shoulders in thick rivers. It oozed down her bodice. It leached into her skirt. Her wedding frock became turquoise.

Marlene calmly stepped from her chair, walked over to the desk, and picked up the telephone. 'Yes, I'd like to see Doctor as soon as possible. It is a matter of some urgency.'

Looking around her for the last time, she left the salon and hurried home where she packed a small suitcase, being careful to layer the turquoise shantung between cloudy folds of pink tissue, and just as carefully encase toiletries and shoes in separate zippered bags in case of accident. Marlene considered one accident for the day to be quite enough.

She drove through the midmorning streets noticing as she went the swathes of sulphur-coloured leaves lining the curbs and gutters. The houses in her suburb were well tended, a fact which Marlene found comforting. She parked the car directly in front of the surgery, removed her suitcase and deftly locked the vehicle. Dropping her keys down the storm water drain on the corner she stood at the front door of the surgery, pressed the bell twice and entered the waiting room.

Marlene knew she looked somewhat dishevelled with half her hair sectioned into serpentine painted locks and her dress the colour it could have been on her wedding day.

'Mrs Gilmore...' said the nurse, but Marlene's eyes forbade her to continue.

'Please tell Doctor I am here, and I wish to see him immediately.'

She passed into a sensible consulting room and placed her suitcase on the examining table before she sat down on the chair she had sat in for many years, opposite the wall displaying Doctor Watersmith's framed certificates.

Within moments he was at her side, dexterously holding a scalpel above her shoulder. Marlene could not have pinpointed the exact moment the blade made contact with the seam, she could only feel the angel skin slipping away from her pale flesh at first quite timorously and then in a quickening surge as it tumbled and cascaded over her breasts, over her hips, over her buttocks, there to lay in a mound of pearls, tulle and taffeta. She stepped out of the frock, mindful not to catch it with her heel, and stood facing the doctor. He smiled and she gripped him firmly by the hand.

'Thank you, Doctor. Please send the account on.'

Marlene opened her suitcase and laid out the turquoise shantung. She spent several moments thoughtfully noting the length of the back zipper. She estimated it to be a full twenty-two inches. Raising the sheath above her head she dropped it down and quickly slid the zipper along the length of her back to her neck. She slid her arms into the jacket and placed the matching netted hat over her pasted hair. She closed the suit-case, picked it up, and walked out through the waiting room and onto the street. Once outside, she strolled to the bus-stop relishing the feel of autumn air on her legs which for so long had been swallowed in the folds of a wedding frock.

14

Moving On

The first I saw of her was when she pulled her black Mercedes into our driveway. After busying herself with some paperwork and a phone call, she got out and walked up to our front door. She knocked three times and waited. I opened the door. She was taller than me, lips shined pink, black heels. A drift of Chanel No. 5.

'Good afternoon, Mr and Mrs Dockerty. My name is Madeleine Hudson from Moving Places Realty. Please take my card. I'm going to personally guide you through this very thrilling time in your lives. May I come in?' She proffered her hand sporting a flawless French manicure.

'I'm Peg and this is Barry,' I said, gesturing to my husband, after my hand had been released from her firm double-handed shake.

My husband said, 'G'day.'

Having made the decision for one reason and another to move closer to my husband's parents, we were selling our house. Madeleine was assigned by the agency to handle everything on our behalf. Would do her best, she assured us, to attract a buyer prepared to pay even more than we would expect as buyers were currently shelling out top dollar for properties. A person or persons, or a couple, perhaps married, maybe not, possibly heterosexual although homosexual was fine too; provided whoever turned out in the end to be the successful purchaser could raise the stakes higher than any other would-be successful purchasers at the Saturday afternoon auction to be held on a day that did not clash with the Grand Final, easy because everyone knows the date of the Grand Final, and always has done, especially now that the rules have changed to allow the ten minute play off in the event of tied scores on the final siren, so there is never again going to be the chance of a Grand Final occurring in October; or the election, which is a bit harder to pin down as no one knows the date, yet everyone has a view as to when it may or should or probably will occur; or the Caulfield Cup, or the Saturday preceding the Melbourne Cup, which, when you think about it, does not leave many Saturdays in Spring, the absolute best time of the year in Melbourne to put a property on the market, before the hot north wind blows in.

Madeleine was going to work with us to pinpoint a date and we needed her realty know-how to nail that perfect day when the greatest number of would-be successful purchasers would arrive in our street, right outside our house, where the auctioneer would oversee them as they waved their hand or raised a finger, or even an eyebrow, while my husband and I sat in the kitchen, ready to decide at what precise moment to allow the auctioneer to announce that the property was on the market. This single day would result in my husband and I becoming purchasers in turn, traipsing through other suburbs, gawping at interiors, planning re-decorations, calculating overall borrowings on the run, and then, after we emerged as the successful purchasers, pack all our belongings into boxes and bags, find new schools for our daughters, a new park in which to walk the dog, and a new hardware shop and café, set close enough to our new house that a quick trip could take in shopping for the bits we would need to make our new house, home, a latte or chai, and a quick glance at the Saturday paper to check that both the price we were paid and the price we paid, remained defensible.

There would be a billboard with top strip lighting so potential purchasers, even those driving by at night, could see inside our house; a dedicated page on movingplacesrealty.com with 360 degree panoramic views of the main rooms; a house plan, also printed on the back of the glossy full colour brochure; ten open days, minimum; and a guarantee of vigorous competition and spirited bidding to make us winners on the day.

After that was agreed to, Madeleine wanted to know what we thought was a reasonable budget. By this she meant how much did my husband and I intend to spend on last-minute touch ups, minor repairs, the garden - front and rear, fresh flowers for at least three rooms, a bowl of crisp green apples bought weekly to offset the kidskin, white swan and tahini colours of the kitchen, which we had only ever thought of as beige in three shades, and three, possibly five, Missoni scatter cushions for our family room.

Madeleine enquired if we had a coffee machine, or if we knew of someone who owned a coffee machine, as she assured my husband and I that something as uncomplicated as the smell of ground coffee brewing can add as much as ten thousand dollars to a sale and imagine what we could do with an extra ten thousand dollars in our new property. 'Smell is just so important,' she purred, 'primal, really. You know, I read the other day it's one of the first things we do as humans. Apparently, as soon as we're born, we smell our mothers, and the memory of that smell never leaves us. Can you believe that?' she said, but before I could tell her that dogs are also very smell-oriented beings, she mentioned that, of course, the dog would not be allowed in the house for the duration of the campaign, as the period between now and the yet to be determined auction date, was now referred to as.

'I know you'll understand that not all people will feel exactly the same way as you do about your dog,' she said, then when she saw the disappointment on my face, was quick to add, 'oh but, look who's a cutesy wootsie poochie!' This, while attempting to air pat our seven-year-old Jack Russell-Staffy cross who had never once in her entire seven years on earth been called cute. 'Basically, in my experience, most people, even doggy people, can't abide someone else's doggy smell.' She screwed her nose up to her eyebrows to illustrate her meaning.

She moved on to our mantelpiece and handed my husband the photos of our daughters taken on their first day at school, the portrait shots and our oldest girl as a debutant, looking prettier than any star of the screen or footballer's wife. Our wedding photo, my parents on board the Nordic Explorer before dad had his fatal heart attack, my husband's parents, my husband's grandmother, my husband's twin sister, my husband's brother and his family, my husband's first dog, a pencil, the miniature watercolour we bought on our honeymoon in Byron Bay, three ballpoint pens, a football fixture for the 2022 season, a small nut-cracking crocodile, my glasses' case, a school excursion form awaiting my signature, yesterday's newspaper folded over to the crossword, a crystal bud vase without a bud, a decorative clock of German manufacture encased in a glass dome, a plastic box filled with my knitting needles and two paperbacks. All swept into my husband's arms as Madeleine busied herself arranging the family photo we had taken last year and meant to present to my husband's parents at Christmastime but somehow in the fuss and bother of the season we ended up buying a cookery book and a cricket book instead. Added to the armful was a small lidded china dish in which we kept the matches to light the fire, and a willowy green glass vase, too thin and too delicate to hold more than a single bloom. 'There,' she said, 'a lovely, homely feel.' She stepped back as if checking the perspective of a painting, then said, 'Of course, don't go lighting the fire on the open days whatever you do, as no one likes to smell the smoke. I usually recommend to my clients that they buy some of those lovely fat candles, you know, the creamy white ones, in three or four different lengths and pop them in the fireplace. Alight, they look divine, and you know, I've even seen people warming their hands in front of a fireplace where there are candles burning. We're so suggestible, aren't we? Another amazing aspect of what it is to be human, I suppose,' she said, before moving on up the hallway.

She continued to re-arrange our things as she walked from room to room, so that by the time we reached the front door, all surfaces had been recast as smooth, diminutive galleries for one object, or perhaps three, but never just two. My husband and I carried the surplus armfuls of pictures and photos and cards and vases and books and shells and lamps and plates and pot plants and other assorted objects, some decorative, some utilitarian, to the kitchen bench. 'Oh, you'll find a temporary home for those,' Madeleine said confidently, 'but don't just put them in a cupboard, because the very first thing any potential purchaser will do, is open the doors on all the built-in cupboards and pull out each and every drawer, and the very last thing they will want to see is a jumble,' she said, with particular emphasis on the words 'first' and 'last'. 'Messy cupboards, in my experience, invariably lead to speculation about house maintenance.' I looked at my husband and then at the ceiling, where we both detected for the first time, and at the same time, a fine crack that ran from the light fitting to the corner of the ornate cornice, reserved solely for the hallway in our house. Madeleine followed my eyes and was quick to say, 'Oh, that's nothing that a bit of filler, a light sand and a quick coat of paint won't fix.' In fact, she went on to say that in our case, the maintenance looked entirely adequate, resulting in perhaps the best-maintained property she had seen for some time.

In a few weeks my husband and I expected that everything we owned would be boxed and bagged waiting to be transported to our new house. Sleep on that first night would not be easy, I imagined. A new house with its unfamiliar corners that would rear up and knock against a shin or an elbow on the way to the bathroom at twenty-past-two in the morning may take some getting used to. But my husband and I had decided. We were selling our house. 'You won't regret this,' Madeleine said. That's exactly what Madeleine had said, that first day. 'You won't regret this.' I went to the hardware shop and picked up two dozen boxes and made a start on packing the non-essentials, which as far as I know are still exactly where I put them, validating if nothing else their non-essential classification.

My husband and I tidied the garden, front and rear, cut back the climbing rose along the side fence, trimmed the camellia near the front door in case an unexpected rainstorm was to pass through just before open day causing the leaves to shower our potential purchasers with cold wet drops. We mowed the lawn, trimmed the edges, and mulched the beds laid barren by years of poor rainfall. We arranged flowers and apples and candles and my husband's sister lent us her coffee maker, which filled the kitchen with minuscule aromatic hisses, each of which bounced and burst its way down the hallway, there to greet our potential purchasers as they crossed the threshold. The beds were made-up with fresh linen, new colour coordinated towels hung in the bathrooms and the three red and two black Missoni cushions cornered the couch and the single armchair. The photographer stood in our rooms and took hundreds of digital photographs and several short videos which he later uploaded to a website so our potential purchasers could walk around our house just as if they were really there, when in actual fact they were sitting in their office, or their home, or even in a café. Of course, they couldn't smell the coffee and the flowers. That's what open days were for.

'It's so invigorating,' said Madeleine after our fifth open day, 'two couples are very keen and I'm working on another potential, as well. He's such an interesting fellow. Works nearby. You might have seen him around even. I've got a feeling that he might just be the one,' she said, 'I really do. He's hot, too,' and she giggled.

In all, we had ten open days, six of which fell on a weekend, when my husband and I arranged for ourselves, our daughters and the dog to be elsewhere for the two-hour period when our potential purchasers would come tramping through the front gate, up the verandah steps, through the front door and on down the hallway until they reached the back door and made their way out to the garden before stopping off in the three bdrms all with BIRs, ensuite to master, roomy bathrm, sep toilet, formal lounge/dining with marble OFP, sep study, kitchen/family with granite benchtops and Bosch appliances, laundry/hobby space, AC, heating, entertainment deck and landscaped rear garden perfect for young families and professionals. Lock-up two car garage doubling as men's retreat, was how the shed was described. That accounted for the fridge, wall mounted television and the old couch my husband had set up so that the dog and he could stretch out together and take in a Sunday afternoon footy game.

On all those weekend open days, bar the last, we walked to our nearby strip, tied the dog to a chair leg and ordered a late breakfast or late lunch from the blackboard. On the last day my husband drove across town to keep an appointment, our eldest daughter was away at her end of season netball trip, and our youngest was at her best friend's birthday party. That left me and the dog to wander down to the shops on our own and order the usual.

Around about three, I untied the dog, and we strolled the short distance back to the house. Madeleine's car was parked in the driveway behind my car. I knocked on the front door, not wanting to disturb her, just in case she was engaged in restrained negotiations with one or other of the potential purchasers, and I suppose, if I think about it now, knocking was a way of announcing myself so as not to give her a start. I turned the knob and pushed open the door. I realised the dog was still with me, so I walked to the side gate and put the dog in the back. I returned to the front and walked down the hallway. I could not see Madeleine anywhere. I called out, 'Hello, Madeleine, I'm home. It's me, Peg,' or words to that effect. There was no reply. The coffee machine was still pulsing out its warm smells and the candles burned brightly in the fireplace. A single apple core, browning in the air, sat on the otherwise clear kitchen bench. I picked it up and moved around the bench, intending to put the core in the bin where it belonged, and that is when I saw Madeleine. She was stretched out full-length on the floor. Her black skirt was dragged up over her head. A few feet away lay articles of clothing including undies, a slip petticoat, and a shoe. I pulled her skirt down and saw that fastened tight around her neck was one of the dog's leads, which usually hung on a hook screwed into the wall near the back door.

After my husband and our girls came home, and after the police, the forensics team, the coroner, several news crews, and a bevy of concerned neighbours left, we shut the door.

'I think we should light a fire,' said my husband, 'it's chilled off considerably.'

I took the candles out from the grate, and he screwed up the real estate pamphlets left on the kitchen bench, brought in some kindling and logs, while I made us a whiskey sour. The girls fished out the photographs of our family and arranged them across the mantlepiece. The dog came in and stretched out before the fire on his favourite cushion. The next morning, we bought a replacement lead and found a new place to hang it behind the laundry door.

15 █

Making Cake

I am sitting in a wedge of sunshine nibbling at a slice from a dead woman's cake. Last Christmas, my friend made chocolate pan forte, and presented me with two slabs. It is more than twelve months since she died, and I am still tripping over the reality that she is no longer here. You see, she killed herself and left a will making me her executor. I have never had this role before.

Her phone rang out. Again and again and again. I went to her place. I stood on the front porch, sheltering from a bitter Saturday morning's weather and rang her bell, hammered on her door, peered in her front window.

Then I dialled 000. Two quiet officers came. They asked me questions. They door-knocked the neighbours. They climbed over the side fence and found her dog locked in the house with oodles of food and water.

I decide to make a cake. I find a recipe for the pan forte I have made these last two years in preference to the usual fruit cake taught to me by my mother, also a dead woman. Mum was 85 when she suffered a heart attack on her way to the kitchen. Her doctor said she would have been gone before she hit the floor, such was the ferocity of the attack. His words, meant kindly, haven't stopped me from thinking about what her last microsecond of consciousness might have been. Did she curse that I was not there to get her a glass of water or whatever it was she was on her way to fetch? Did she wonder why I could never love her in the way she wanted to be loved, deserved to be loved, by an only daughter? All I know is she never had another thought or feeling. She died alone, on the floor, on her way to the kitchen.

Mothers and daughters. These relationships take many forms and are never as they might be or could be. Or should be. Some are desultory affairs with a minimum of deference where some occasions are marked, but not all. Others are warm and close with love passing between the pair like a young boy's electronics model conducts electricity. Then there are those that are stifling and exclusive, leaving not much room for husbands, children, siblings, friends.

On the night my friend died, I sat in the reading chair in front of the fire. I admit I had too much to drink but it wasn't an ordinary Saturday evening. Several bottles of wine had evaporated over the dinner I shared with my husband, my daughter, my son and some of the grandchildren. My daughter sat with me, long after the others had left or gone to bed and as we talked, the talk became bitter.

'When my friends told me how lucky I was to have you to

help when I had the twins, I felt like telling them the truth,' she said. 'I've never been good enough for you, and you're never happy about anything I do.'

She went on, I listened. I sobbed. It had been a long time between tears for me. I said some stuff when I could get the breath. I'm sure we did not mend our fences. Or if we did, it was only a temporary fix.

My mother and I never spoke to each other like that. In fact, my mother and I never spoke to each other much at all. She was a woman whose grief, bottled and corked, had entered her world long before I came along. I don't know if she shared her grief with my father. Perhaps. I do know she never shared it with me.

Notwithstanding the grief, she did share most everything else. When I was seven, she let me make a two-minute chocolate cake that was one of her signature dishes whenever she needed a cake for the shearers' morning tea, or the guild meeting, or to take to the football. On this occasion my brother needed a cake to take to a high school social, back in the days when kids were not embarrassed to bring a sponge or a dozen eggs to school to help with fund raising for a swimming pool or a new library. The two-minute chocolate cake is very easy to make, true to its name, and I will let you into its secrets in a little while.

There were agricultural shows that she encouraged me to embrace. We went to all the shows in the district because my father showed his fine wool merino sheep. We had a leather suitcase full of ribbons those sheep won, as well as two photos hanging in the sitting room, a champion ewe, and a champion ram. The photos were hand-coloured and hung beside mum and dad's wedding photo, also hand-coloured.

Mum, who had once entered her cooking and preserves and award-winning flowers in shows, preferred to help me while she worked in the kitchen making lunch or afternoon tea for the men, who worked outdoors and needed feeding. I learnt to make her half-pound fruit cakes, plain scones, sponge cakes, drop biscuits, queen cakes, rock cakes and other things too, such as her delicious sausage rolls, the like of which I have never tasted since. 1964 was a bumper year. I won three firsts and a second at Natimuk, another three firsts and a second at Edenhope, and four firsts and a second at Penola.

'What are these tickets for, Granny?' asked my granddaughter one evening before dinner, as she was leafing through a recipe book made by me when I was a girl. I explained the show thing and she said, 'I want to enter stuff, too.' We found a show not far north of Ballarat, and sent away for the schedule.

'It's here,' she yelled week or so later, as she fished her hand into the letterbox and pulled out a thick envelope addressed to her. We bent our heads over the close-typed 48 pages and marked the categories she might have a go at. 'Don't know about the decorated cake idea, though,' I said. 'My father used to do all the decorations on mum's cakes because he had a steady hand. Our dining table was covered in royal-icing rose buds and frills for weeks. It took ages to get one of those cakes finished.'

On the day of the show, the alarm went off at six. 'Time

to get up and hit the road,' I said, gulping down a cup of tea in the hope it would keep me awake long enough to drive the 150kms west. We got there just in time to shove her entries through the door before the home-crafts pavilion closed for judging.

'What are we going to do now?' It was eight-thirty and already threatening to be hot. Dust blew along the roadside as we returned to the car with the empty containers.

'Let's get a drink and look at the animals,' she said, and for the next three hours we visited every animal on display. We liked the birds of prey demonstration and cheered on a creamy-coloured ferret. It was one of four creatures shoved into lengths of plastic piping by its owner, a member of the Victorian Ferret Society, in the hope that it would emerge at the other end victorious. The ferret that is, not the owner, most of whom were far too rotund to slide through a narrow doorway let alone crawl down a length of pipe. We loved the Border Collie pups, three black and white beauties that rolled over for tummy rubs and tumbled over each other in the rush to get patted, as well as the auburn tressed Scottish highland cattle. Their owners gave them bucket after bucket of water.

At midday the pavilion door opened. I knew the time to the second. 'Want to see if the judges are finished?'

'Granny! There's a ticket near the bread,' she yelled. I quickened my pace and saw the tickets, not one, but two, awarding this high-tin loaf of perfect white bread, sliced in half to see if it was doughy or full of air holes, first prize and a special award for a champion exhibit.

'Hell, that's fantastic.'

She won first prizes for her egg and bacon pie and her sausage rolls. The sponge cake did not fare so well. Still, not bad for an eleven-year-old in her first show. Her mother arrived a few minutes later with the twins in tow and hugged her until she was half-squeezed.

'Let me see,' yelled the twins together, and so we trooped through the pavilion again, admiring the flash blue and red cards with her name printed on them.

We spent the afternoon watching the wood chop and the sheep shearing competition, slurping icy poles, playing on the new tractor displays and going on the ghost train. At five we collected the winning produce along with the few dollars and packets of flour, additional prizes donated by the local shops and patrons, and headed back down the highway.

I return to the kitchen and make another cup of tea and take it outside with my recipe book. I turn to my mother's recipe for half-pound fruit cake written in her hand on a piece of writing paper that I have glued into my book. It calls for half a pound of the key ingredients, butter, and sugar, which must be thoroughly creamed before adding five eggs, separately, and beating well after each addition. If the mixture begins to curdle, it is possible to add a tablespoon of the 10 ounces of plain flour that must be double sifted with two teaspoons of mixed spice, a teaspoon of nutmeg and a teaspoon of cinnamon. After that, add a tablespoon or two of either treacle – if you want a dark fruit cake – or Golden Syrup – if a lighter version is required, and a dash of vanilla or lemon essence, whatever your fancy.

Several days before you do all this you need to soak one and a half pounds of mixed fruit in sherry or brandy. Use a mixture of sultanas, currants, raisins, mixed peel and cherries. Not those awful pretend cherries, but real glacé ones. Not that it's in my mother's recipe, but these days I add glacé ginger and almonds, too, as I like these flavours on my tongue.

Before you mix the wet ingredients, you must line a 22cm round tin with several layers of brown paper, finished off with a layer of baking paper. This protects the cake from its hours in the oven. You can of course double this recipe and make two cakes. I often do. Set the oven to about 150 degrees and pop the cake in, not up the top, but in the middle of the oven. It will take about 3 hours to cook. If it begins to crack on the top, cover it over loosely with a piece of foil or baking paper – not tight as you don't want to trap steam, mind. You can test if it's cooked by stabbing the middle with a skewer or a strand of straw taken from a broom. You are looking for evidence of an uncooked middle. Of course, soggy fruit can mimic soggy cake.

When the cake is ready, take it out of the oven and leave it to cool in the tin overnight. The next day, turn it out and wrap it in layers of baking paper followed by several sheets of newspaper and put it away until it is ready to be cracked, perhaps during Christmas week to accompany some sparkling white wine or a Spanish sherry, or a fine cup of tea served on your best China. Sometimes I brush the cake with brandy before I wrap it up. If you like, you can skewer the cake and drift a little brandy into the holes.

This cake is best made two or three months before you want to eat it and will keep at least a year after cooked and cut.

Oh, and by the way, for the half pound cake, 250 grams is approximately half a pound or eight ounces. And before I forget, here's the recipe for the two-minute chocolate cake.

Set the oven to 180 degrees and grease and line the base of two 22mm round cake tins. In a bowl – electric mixer bowl preferably – place 2 tablespoons of cocoa sifted with 2 cups of self-raising flour and 1 ½ cups of sugar. Melt two table-spoons of butter – butter, not margarine – and add it to the dry ingredients along with 2 eggs and 1 ½ cups of milk. Beat for 2 minutes – hence the name – then pour equal amounts into the two tins. Bake for approximately 30 minutes, and test in the same way as you would for the half pound fruit cake. Turn onto a wire rack covered with a clean tea towel and peel off the paper lining. Wait until it's cool then sandwich together with icing or cream – add strawberries or cherries for instance, and ice the top. You could use coffee icing and sprinkle chopped walnuts on top, too. This cake keeps well for five or so days and is best eaten with a cup of tea. You can also cook it in patty pan cases, but you will need to shorten the time in the oven.

In the next few weeks, I must pen an affidavit in answer to whatever will be in the affidavit of my friend's father. He is contesting her will on the grounds she had an obligation to support him. Funny that. He allowed her to be made a ward of the state when her mother was murdered as he continued to drink his way through adulthood into old age. And he never phoned her when she fled as far away from America as she could, after finishing college. On her few trips back to the States, she came back defeated and dishevelled. 'I'm not going again,' she said the last time. 'I don't need the lectures anymore. Never did need them.'

In contrast, I will need a good fruit cake and many cups of tea to work my way through this stage of the death cycle.

Acknowledgements

These stories have been written over time, reviewed, redrafted and rehashed. Those who have provided advice and feedback have no doubt forgotten that they did so, it being so long ago in some instances. However, perhaps the first real feedback was given by Carmel Bird for the story, 'One Conversation with my Husband'. I cherish her comments and insights. Making sure I've applied her dictums and my learning is another matter, and in no way is Carmel to blame if you find some of the stories in here silly or sloppy or solipsistic.

Bruce Pascoe was an early reader of 'Going to Folkestone'. He considered it good enough but not good enough to publish in Australian Stories. I recall having an audience with him in Ballarat and so wishing he would say yes. But sadly, he didn't.

Other stories have travelled here and there, one winning a prize or something like that. Friends have read some, and I've read some out loud to audiences. No one has really known what to say. Isn't that always the case?

I thank the dexterous writers I know and especially those with whom I have joined forces in assorted and sundry writing courses and workshops. It's been terrific fun and the best way to improve.

Janice Simpson lives and works in regional Victoria. She writes crime novels, mostly, and reads anything that's worth reading. Actually, she fits writing in these days due to a calendar full of building bike trails and organising local word festivals.